THE CARDINAL'S
ASSASSIN

Other titles by Donald Cozzens

Nonfiction

Notes from the Underground
Freeing Celibacy
Faith That Dares to Speak
Sacred Silence: Denial and the Crisis in the Church
The Changing Face of the Priesthood
The Spirituality of the Diocesan Priest (Editor)

Fiction

Master of Ceremonies
Under Pain of Mortal Sin

THE CARDINAL'S ASSASSIN

DONALD COZZENS

in extenso

THE CARDINAL'S ASSASSIN
by Donald Cozzens

Edited by Michael Coyne
Design and typesetting by Patricia A. Lynch
Cover images: These files by Alekjds are licensed under the Creative
Commons Attribution-Share Alike 3.0 Unported license.

Photo of Donald Cozzens by Paul Tepley

Published by In Extenso Press, an imprint of ACTA Publications,
4848 N. Clark Street, Chicago, IL 60640, (800) 397-2282,
actapublications.com

This story is fiction. Aside from references to well-known historic figures,
any similarity to actual people, living or dead, is purely coincidental.

Library of Congress Catalog Number: 2021933483
ISBN: 978-0-87946-696-1 (hardcover)
ISBN: 978-0-87946-695-4 (paperback)
Printed in the United States of America by Total Printing Systems
Year 35 34 33 32 31 30 29 28 27 26 25 24 23 22 21
Printing 15 14 13 12 11 10 9 8 7 6 5 4 3 2 First

♻ Text printed on 30% post-consumer recycled paper

To
Cardinal Michael L. Fitzgerald, M.Afr.,
humble scholar and bridge builder
between Christianity and Islam

Men never do evil so completely and cheerfully as when they do it from religious conviction.

Blaise Pascal

1

Giorgio Grotti stepped out of the shower after a late-morning run. Physically he was at his prime, but in his heart he was off center, edgy, and restless. His cramped quarters on the lowest level of the episcopal palace were just a part of it. He was, to all appearances, little more than hired help—the archbishop's driver. Nor could he accept that he had no place at the archbishop's table.

Before he could dress, he heard a staccato rap on the door. Grotti wrapped his towel around his waist and, annoyed, moved to the door. It was Simon Ashley, the effete curator of the archbishop's extensive collection of Renaissance art. Grotti didn't much like Ashley—he found him smug and condescending— and it was clear that Ashley thought him an intellectual and cultural inferior.

"The archbishop would like to see you. Now. He's in his study." Ashley turned on his heel and walked away without waiting for Grotti's response.

Cardinal-elect Pietro Gonzaga Montaldo, Archbishop of Perugia, moved slowly to his desk with the resolve of a Napoleon planning his next battle.

"By the grace of God, Giorgio, we have been given a second chance to rectify the American threat against our wounded, vulnerable church." Montaldo eased himself into his high-back desk chair while motioning to Grotti to take a wingtip leather chair in front of the desk. Without staring, the archbishop took in the lean yet muscled body of his chauffeur—and enforcer—dressed, as usual, in a dark suit and open-necked shirt. With his middle finger, Montaldo pushed his rimless glasses up the bridge of his nose, catching the scent of Grotti's cologne. He smiled to himself. Some in Rome, certainly his patrons, Cardinal Alessandro Vinnucci and Cardinal Andrea Oradini, suspected Grotti was his love toy. Of course those two, and others in the Vatican, would presume that. The truth was that the relationship with his "chauffeur" was coldly professional, though disguised for Grotti's sake in the language of piety and loyalty to the church. Montaldo closed his eyes for a moment. *Poor Giorgio. A loyal and skilled soldier, but he had little idea of the scope of the struggle he had enlisted in, a war for the soul of the Catholic Church.* The archbishop raised his head and met the eyes of his private assassin, the former seminarian and renegade carabiniere. Though Grotti had failed to complete his last assignment—the elimination of an American bishop who had stumbled upon Montaldo's secret societies—this time, with the help of God, he would succeed.

"A second chance, Archbishop?" Grotti took Montaldo's "second chance" for what it was—a subtle rebuke for his bungling of the assassination of Bishop Bryn Martin, the new Ordinary of Cleveland and a protégé and confidant of Cardinal-elect Charles Cullen, the current Archbishop of Baltimore. Grotti knew where this was going. His boss thought of Cullen and Martin as soft, slinking liberals, excited by the current, always dangerous, winds of ecclesial change. Seduced by the liberation theologies stoked by the Vatican Council, these two prelates, and scoundrels like them, were naively open to the reform movements destroying Montaldo's church. And his boss would do whatever was necessary to restore the Church of Rome to its destiny as the supreme spiritual power the world over. But Grotti suspected the deeper, more urgent reason for the assassination of these American prelates was fear. They knew too much about the operations—and financing—of Montaldo's secret societies, his Brotherhood of the Sacred Purple and Sentinels of the Supreme Center.

"I've prayed, Giorgio, that I might find another way. But I'm afraid the elimination of Bishop Martin and Archbishop Cullen is unfortunately necessary." Montaldo lowered his eyes. "Necessary for the success of our sacred mission."

Giorgio Grotti lifted his shoulders and sat up in his chair as if rising to attention. His assignment came veiled, as usual, under Montaldo's professed distaste for the perhaps regrettable, but necessary, elimination of enemies of the church. The archbishop bore an alert yet expressionless countenance, a face Grotti himself had learned to wear as a carabiniere. But he registered his employer's feigned regret while ordering assassinations as no more than sanctimonious theater. Cardinal-elect Pietro Montaldo was as cold-blooded as they came. Grotti lowered his eyes and eased slightly back into his chair. Since moving from Rome to Perguia, he had seen how his boss lived—swallowing in greedy gulps the privileges of his episcopal appointment. While Montaldo had the flint-hard will of a warrior, he lived like a spoiled prince, indulging his taste for the best of Italian art, the finest of Italian wine, the company of the wealthiest men of Rome and now Perugia. Yes, Grotti was ready to accept this "second-chance" assignment. But perhaps not quite as ready as he had been when the archbishop first recruited him as his secret operative. *How was I so easily seduced?* He took a deep breath, held it for a moment, then looked up at Montaldo. "I under-stand," was all he said.

The Archbishop-Prince of Perugia studied the pensive eyes of his private assassin. The split-second hesitation he sensed was so unlike Grotti.

"What is it, Giorgio? Something bothering you?"

Grotti gave his archbishop a half smile and again hesitated a few telling seconds. "When I was expelled from the seminary, the rector told me that I had serious anger issues. Maybe he was right."

"You might think of your anger as…" Montaldo assumed the pose of a wise and understanding mentor…"as righteous anger, even holy anger. Anger employed by God for the safeguarding of his church. You are on a sacred mission, Giorgio, a mission only the most committed to the church can understand."

Grotti nodded and murmured softly, "Of course. Please con-tinue, Archbishop."

"As you know, the joy of my recent election to the College of Cardinals was, shall we say, damped when I saw that Archbishop Cullen was to receive the red hat at the same consistory. How could this be? My cohorts in the curia have failed me."

Grotti nodded. Did his boss really think that Vannucci and Oradini and their ilk controlled who was named to the College of Cardinals?

Then, with the merest hint of a smile, the archbishop con-tinued, "I have been informed that Bishop Martin will be accom-panying Archbishop Cullen to Rome for the consistory. A light shines in the darkness. The heretics, you see, Giorgio, will be coming to us. How convenient for you. No need for further trips to Baltimore or Cleveland."

Grotti, his thick hands now resting on the arms of his chair, read the condescending look in the archbishop's eyes—*You will, of course, succeed this time.* Yes, he was growing tired of the man's arrogance, his self-righteous confidence that he alone had discovered the true enemies of the church and that he had the right—no, the obligation—to order their assassinations.

Grotti chided himself for ruminating like an old lady worrying about the sins of her youth. But he couldn't shake the thought. He had been paid very well for his services to the archbishop. He was now a rich man, and perhaps it was time to execute the early retirement he had long been contemplating. Suddenly everything seemed clear to him. This assignment, the assassination of Cullen and Martin, would be the last time he would kill for the good of Holy Mother Church.

Giorgio Grotti found himself almost surprised by his own words. "I will not fail you, *Eminenza.*" While Montaldo was not yet officially a cardinal, Grotti had always recognized the archbishop's extreme pleasure when his staff addressed him with honorifics.

The cardinal-elect stood slowly, and before turning his back to Grotti said, "*Vade in pace*"—go in peace. Montaldo walked to the window of his study. His driver had been dismissed.

2

Grotti left the archbishop's palace through the servants' entrance and walked slowly, but with his mind racing, toward the bars and coffee shops that skirted Perugia's cathedral and episcopal palace. He ordered an espresso at the first outdoor table he found open. This new assignment would be difficult. These consistories, these rites of making new cardinals, turned the streets and hotels of Rome—especially those close to the Vatican—into little circuses. The streets came alive with the joyful but restrained partying of family and friends who had traveled to Rome to celebrate with the new princes of the church. But perhaps he could use the carnival-like atmosphere to his advantage. Grotti knew he was good at this—plotting often difficult operations in careful detail. He would have to be at the very top of his game to execute this, his final assignment. The adrenaline rush he felt rising in his veins seemed to assuage his discomfort about Montaldo's easy turn to violence in safeguarding his secret holy war to protect the church of Jesus Christ.

Against his will, he slipped back into the thoughts he had hidden from Montaldo less than an hour ago. He was in his late thirties now and still as fit as he had been in his twenties. To his friends in Rome—friends he seldom saw since his move to Perugia—he was just a bishop's driver and low-level assistant. How could they possibly understand why he had left an elite branch of the Carabinieri to work for a bishop? Maybe one day he would be able to tell his social circle he had been much more than a chauffeur. If they only knew that their friend, Giorgio Grotti, was not a mere personal assistant to a single cleric, but a special operative for a discreet corps of clerics charged with the protection of the true faith of the Catholic Church. And like James Bond of MI-6, who had a license to kill, Grotti had a *dispensation* to kill—*Ad majorem Dei gloriam.* The thought always amused him. But he knew his real work as Montaldo's assassin would have to remain his secret for the rest of his life. He squeezed his eyes closed and told himself he should be proud of his special role in purging the church of dangerous heretics. A lie? Perhaps. But it was a lie that had always soothed him in the past.

Grotti's reverie shifted to his mother as the waiter brought a second espresso. She would never know that what her son was doing was far more important than being a parish priest. He gazed into his cup and wondered: What if, as a young seminarian, he had not broken the nose of a classmate who had tried to fondle him? What if he had not joined the Carabinieri and made his way into their Special Intervention Group? And what if he had not gone to confession to Archbishop Montaldo or had declined his invitation to join his secret war? Grotti might be happier but—suppressing a twinge of guilt—he admitted to himself that he had never felt more alive than when on assignment as Montaldo's assassin.

A handsome priest wearing a cassock slowed as he passed his table and smiled. Grotti was flattered...and felt his stomach tighten.

He pushed his chair back, stood gracefully, paid the check, and walked aimlessly down Via Vincioli, past the Primavera Hotel, a favorite of tourists eager to visit Perugia's Cattedrale di San Lorenzo. The afternoon sun warmed the shoulders of his tailored black suitcoat, accented the sheen of his white, open-necked shirt. Tall for an Italian, Grotti took quiet pleasure in his wiry frame. Some of the women he passed on the street of charcoal-colored stone held his glance a second longer than normal, a passing glance that on any other day might have lead to a flirtation, perhaps an assignation. But to his surprise he felt unfocused and distracted in spite of the quickening in his loins. Ordinarily an assignment from Montaldo, the kind he had received only an hour ago, would focus his energy and sharpen his thinking. But not today. Instead of the initial planning and plotting necessary to execute the assassinations, he found himself thinking about Montaldo's new master of ceremonies, the stuffy Englishman, Father Trace Dunmore, and Montaldo's recently hired curator of the cathedral's collection of religious art, the Oxford-educated fop, Simon Ashley. Both men, to Grotti's surprise, had arrived suddenly from Cleveland, Ohio, where Dunmore had for a brief time been on Bishop Bryn Martin's chancery staff and Ashley had held an academic post in the art history department at John Carroll, the Jesuit university there. Montaldo had never explained their presence, but Grotti, smiling to himself, knew they were on the run—and why—and that the archbishop was giving them cover. From their first days in the palace, he hadn't liked the arrangement. Ashley for sure, and probably Dunmore, had narrowly escaped arrest as accomplices in the attempted murder Grotti himself had botched. He had killed a decoy instead of his assigned target, Bishop Bryn Martin.

Grotti knew from the housekeeping and kitchen staff that the evening meals in Montaldo's dining room lasted much longer now that the archbishop had their company. Mostly, he was told, they talked about Montaldo's art collection and what clerical gossip made its way north from the Vatican.

It was also clear to Grotti that both Dunmore and Ashley were members of the archbishop's secret societies of well-placed clergy and wealthy laity supporting his mission. He knew that Ashley and Dunmore had recruited a retired Cleveland cop to kill, for the good of the church, of course, several women claiming extraordinary ordination to the priesthood.

The English snobs strutted around the palace like Montaldo's favorite sons—and they barely acknowledged Grotti's presence in the household. It placated him a little to know that his monthly stipend was three times higher than theirs. Still, their very presence in Perugia irked him. Not just because they were such effete homosexuals but because they had the archbishop's ear...and no doubt knew secrets he was not privy to.

3

Rome, late afternoon

Giorgio Grotti found a parking space on the street almost directly in front of the Ristorante Carlo in the Trastevere district of Rome. He had told his boss that he needed to spend some time close to the Vatican to plan the assassinations. Emerging from the archbishop's black Audi, and feeling stiff from the two-hour drive from Perugia, he ambled first toward the men's room in the back of the nearly empty restaurant. He sat alone at the bar a few minutes later, waiting for Angelo Correa, like himself, a former carabiniere. But instead of working for the church, like Grotti, Correa had become an enforcer for the Scarano family. For an operation as dangerous and difficult as he was facing, Grotti would need the assistance of someone like Correa. It would be the first time Grotti ever used an accomplice.

He turned on his bar stool and, looking around the restaurant, caught sight of a man sitting alone in shadow at a corner table. It looked like Correa. The man sat with his back to the wall sipping a red wine and smiled—or was it a sneer?—as Grotti moved toward the table.

"Forgive me, Giorgio, but I wasn't sure it was you. Though you haven't changed much, my friend."

"You look pretty good yourself," Grotti said. "I appreciate your meeting me."

"Well, I was curious about all the rumors I've heard. You were our unit's best marksman, best sniper, and all of a sudden you resign from the Carabinieri and go to work for some goddamn bishop?"

Grotti furrowed his brow, "I know it doesn't seem to make sense, but it's not quite like that. Officially, I'm the driver to the Archbishop of Perugia—soon to be *Cardinal* Pietro Gonzaga Montaldo."

Correa snorted. "The word is you're his personal enforcer in his secret war for the soul of the church. A war that is not as secret as he thinks." Correa sipped his wine and held Grotti's gaze. "You and I," he whispered, "we're much the same. Paid assassins. Men who murder strangers for money. The only difference between us is that you think you piss holy water." Both men laughed.

Over Carlo's featured *rigatoni alla gricia* and a carafe of the house chianti, Grotti described his assignment to take out both Cardinal-elect Charles Cullen and Bishop Bryn Martin.

"Whew," whistled Correa. "What is it with this Montaldo guy?"

"I know, I know. Talk about a savior complex. My boss really thinks he is saving the church from the liberals' slide into heresy. What he calls 'relativism.' Secularism." Grotti went silent a moment before adding, "The failed priest in me signed on."

"I hope Montaldo is paying you well."

"My compensation is commensurate with my talents," Grotti smiled.

"You know, of course, that I work for the Scarano family. For Don Leonine. His inner circle all call him 'Leo,' but I've not made it yet. But soon. I call him 'Padrino.' Scarano is well connected with some of the top cardinals and bishops in the curia and with Vatican bankers and the big-money moguls doing business with the Vatican. From time to time, he mentions your boss."

Grotti felt out of his depth. *Montaldo has mob connections?* His mind raced.

Correa, seeming to sense Grotti's discomfort, added, "He knows him well enough not to like him." Correa smiled. "Maybe they're too much alike."

Grotti nodded as if he understood more than he did. But he was seeing a new side of his boss—a side he didn't like at all.

"Your Montaldo, he's quite a rich man. He goddamn better be paying you well." Correa put his fork down and sat back in his chair.

"I know he's wealthy," Grotti said, leaning across the table. "Come visit me at the bishop's palace in Perugia sometime and you'll see firsthand. I don't know where he gets it all, Angelo, but Cardinals Alessandro Oradini and Andrea Vannucci are two sources he calls on regularly."

Angelo smiled, savoring the pleasure he took in what he was about to reveal. He touched the small accent candle burning in the center of the table, moving it closer to his side. "Of course, he does, Giorgio." Correa lifted his chin, the lines of his face accentuated in the light of the flame, and said, *sotto voce*, "Montaldo is blackmailing both of them."

Grotti sat still, trying to hide his surprise. "What does he have on them?"

"First, tell me what you know about Vannucci."

"Not much," Grotti said, his head swimming with the news of blackmail. "He likes to mention that he is a descendant of the Renaissance painter, Pietro Vannucci, better known as Pietro Perugino. He never fails to add that Raphael himself was a student of Pietro."

"And Oradini?"

"Even less. He and Vannucci, they're longtime friends, members of the old guard, and living like...like aristocrats, like Vatican royalty. They think of themselves as behind-the-scenes players in the politics of the curia. And as silent backers of my boss. They've made a number of trips to Perugia since Montaldo was made archbishop. Always just for dinner. Always to be updated on the work of Montaldo's secret societies. And always leaving envelopes stuffed with cash before heading back to Rome."

Correa smirked. "Well, my friend, let me be your *professore* for a moment. The Scarano family is sitting on a bucket of secrets when it comes to Vannucci and Oradini. For starters, both of the old birds are Masons, and members of the notorious P2 Lodge, a lodge embedded in the Vatican for generations." Correa shrugged, "Perhaps not a mortal sin. But it gets better." He brought his napkin to his lips, smothering a burp. "Their fathers were small but ambitious bankers in Rome during the war." Correa refilled their wine glasses. "This is where it really gets good. After the war, their papas made huge sums of money arranging for the transfer of Nazi officials' funds to select banks in South America, particularly to banks in Asunción in Paraguay. Mr. Vannucci and Mr. Oradini, you see, were *full-service* bankers."

Grotti raised his eyebrows and smiled weakly.

Correa paused for a sip of wine. "They also arranged for visas and passports and letters of introduction for Nazi military officers and their families eager to get out of Europe. And they were paid, as you can imagine, quite well for their efforts."

Grotti leaned back in his chair. "This makes perfect sense. I never quite understood why Oradini and Vannucci seemed so ready to respond when Montaldo needed cash for his secret war machine." He shook his head. "Not now, but one of these days, I'll tell you all about Montaldo's secret societies." *I know a few secrets, too.*

Grotti glanced aimlessly around the restaurant, letting what he had just heard sink in. "If it ever got out that the cardinals' fathers helped Nazi war criminals, their status in the Vatican court would go down the toilet."

"Of course, Giorgio, of course," Correa hesitated, seeming pleased with himself for the education he was giving Grotti. "This...now this I don't know for sure, but Leonine Scarano, the don, believes Oradini's and Vannucci's fathers were spies. Spying during the war for German military intelligence. Just think of it: *Abwehr* spies embedded in the Vatican! Whether or not that's true, their banks did a lot of business with the Vatican in the post-war years and they themselves were often seen in many curial offices. These guys, along with some fat-cat financiers, helped the Vatican set up its own bank, the pious-sounding Institute for Religious Works. That's how they really became wealthy—money laundering and messing in other shady banking deals."

"So their sons, now cardinals of the church, became very wealthy power brokers in the Vatican," Grotti said. What he didn't add was that he knew, he just knew, that Vannucci and Oradini were the ones financing Montaldo's secret societies. Grotti felt as if he was stepping out of some kind of fog. His life as a soldier for Pietro Montaldo was suddenly coming into sharp focus. The Archbishop of Perugia was not quite the noble warrior he made himself out to be. *His sacred mission to save the church is being funded by plundered Nazi fortunes.* Grotti shook his head, trying desperately to focus on the here and now. He had to get back into the moment. And back to the business at hand.

But Correa had still more to reveal about Montaldo. "He likes handsome young seminarians and priests. And he is often looking for male prostitutes, young boys, mostly immigrants from the Mideast."

"Are you serious?" Grotti said, trying to sound calm.

"Of course I am. You know as well as I how many Vatican priests and bishops are gay. Most remain celibate, I guess...or at least they make an effort to remain so. But some barely even try to maintain appearances. And Montaldo is in that crowd. He's careful, but we know he's a player."

Grotti felt blindsided. The man who had given his life a sense of meaning was an active homosexual, one who preyed on young immigrant boys, even young seminarians. He gritted his teeth in silence. He hated what he always called "fags." *Holy Mother of God*, he thought, *who have I been working for all these years?*

Correa was stunned by his friend's sudden change in demeanor. *What was wrong with Giorgio? Didn't he, of all people, know what went on behind the walls of Vatican City?*

With an iron will, Grotti repressed his reaction to what he had just heard. He would deal with it later. But now, now he had to focus. He sat silent, staring at the table. When he lifted his head, back in the moment, he said, "Here's what I need from you, Angelo. And since we have been talking about money, Montaldo's pockets, we know, are deep. He will be generous. So I expect the best. First, some intel. The name of the hotel where Cullen and his party will be staying. The restaurants where they have reservations. The names of the people in his official party. What kind of security Cullen and the new cardinals will have from the Carabinieri, the Polizia di Stato, and the Vatican Gendarmerie."

"None of that will be difficult," Correa bragged.

"Next, some help with the operation itself. I haven't thought it through yet, but I plan to poison Cullen. I'm not sure about Martin. First I need to find someone with access to a reliable, fast-acting toxin."

Correa broke into a wide grin. "One of the family is a pharmacologist. She works at Salvator Mundi Hospital by day. Her name is Vittoria Massi. We've worked together before. She's the best. You'll like her," he said, almost suggestively. "The enemies of the Scarano family fear her more than me. She can get what you need, and if you want, even deliver it directly to the new cardinal and his bishop friend." He studied in silence the other man's reaction to the proposition.

Grotti's eyes widened. "Let me think about that. If she's as good as you say..."

"Giorgio, trust me, this woman delivers."

4

Cleveland, Ohio, East Side, late afternoon.

Sister Celine Mackey sat at the elbow of the bar closest to the front door of Monty's Tavern talking to two young women on adjacent stools. Before her was her signature drink—a tall glass of equal parts club soda and tonic water with a slice of lime. She took a last sip. "Time for me to go. The two sisters I live with pray vespers, our evening prayer, at five. I don't like to be late."

"You go, 'ster... Don't want to be late for your prayers," said the woman next to her with a sodden grin.

"I'll look for you both next week. Maybe at the McDonalds or Burger King. Be careful out there."

Sister Celine slid off her stool, picked up her canvas tote bag emblazoned with "Sisters of Notre Dame, Chardon, Ohio," and walked out onto St. Clair Avenue.

Thirty seconds later, a man at the other end of bar slipped out the back door.

Sister Celine walked toward East 75th and turned at the corner. Her Honda Civic was parked at the curb. As she reached for the door handle, a man grabbed her by her shoulders and turned her around, his face inches from hers.

"Stay away from my girls, bitch. They don't need to hear any God talk, especially from some nun." With his left hand, he squeezed her throat, pushing her hard against the driver-side door of her car. She couldn't scream. She couldn't move. She had nowhere to look but into his watery eyes, streaked with red spider veins. He slapped her face with his open right hand. She saw a bright flash of light. He slapped her again with the back of his hand. This time one of his rings sliced into the nun's right cheek.

"Leave them alone," he snarled, his face back up against hers. "Don't mess with my girls." The pimp abruptly turned and walked to the back entrance of Monty's Tavern.

Sister Celine sat up straight on the gurney in Examining Room 3 in the Emergency Department of University Hospitals, her right cheek bandaged over a few stitches. The cut wasn't deep, but the stitches would minimize scarring. She didn't need anything stronger than Tylenol for the pain, and her nurse said the swelling would be gone in a day or so.

"You're free to go, Sister, as soon as the attending physician has a final look at your chart," the middle-aged nurse said. "Oh, and the police officer outside wants you to sign the statement you gave. He's in the waiting area."

There was a quiet rap at the door. Sister Celine looked up to see the Bishop of Cleveland, Bryn Martin, standing there.

"May I come in?" he said.

"Bishop, you really didn't have to come. I'm going to be fine. Although I do think I'll have a real drink when I get out of here."

Martin laughed. "Yes, a stiff one. Tell me what happened, Sister."

"If you can wait a few minutes, Sister Amelia, my superior, is on her way, and she is going to want to hear the whole story too."

"Of course." The bishop went silent for a moment. "You know, I was told of your ministry to young women caught up in the sex trade soon after I arrived here. Especially now, I'd like to affirm your ministry…and support it in practical ways."

Celine's cheeks colored. "I've learned a lot about survival from these girls—most of them only in their late teens and early twenties. Their stories break my heart."

Martin's eyes softened. "How's the pain level?"

"Not bad. Maybe a one-and-a-half. Ask me again when the Tylenol wears off." They both smiled. "But I was really frightened. I'm still shaking inside."

Bishop and nun both lowered their eyes, the silence only a bit awkward.

"Maybe this moment of waiting was meant to be, Bishop. There's something I've been wrestling with, something I think I should tell you."

Martin offered an encouraging expression. Celine seemed to say a silent prayer. Martin said his own. *Be with her, Holy Spirit.*

She cracked open a bottle of water, twisted the cap off slowly, and took a sip. "Two of the girls tell me that one of their clients is a Catholic priest. They say he's shy. He's kind. Unlike their other johns, he seems embarrassed by the…transaction. The girls think he wants physical intimacy more than sex, mostly to be held in someone's arms, more than just the quick wham bam and be gone."

Martin didn't react.

"I don't know his name. I'm sure the girls don't even know his real name. Although that shouldn't be too hard to find out."

Martin closed his eyes. Celine thought he looked sad, and almost regretted her candor.

"Sister Celine, thank you for trusting me with this. My hunch is that this priest is profoundly lonely, and really unhappy. I would like to help him, not punish him."

Celine lowered her shoulders. "I was hoping you would say something like that. Expected it, even." In the silence that followed, the two connected in a way they had never done before.

"Celine!"

The voice seemed to come out of nowhere and the moment was broken. An older woman rushed up to Celine and hugged her gently.

"I came as soon as you called. Are you okay?"

"I'm going to be fine. Look who's here." Celine turned to Bishop Martin.

Before the woman could speak, Martin said, "Sister Amelia, we haven't had a chance to speak privately, but I remember meeting you when I met with diocesan leaders a few weeks ago." Like Celine, Amelia was tall, five nine or so, and slender, a woman in her middle fifties with evident intelligence in her gaze.

"It's so good of you to come, Bishop." Amelia turned back to Celine. "Tell me what happened."

"I asked Bishop Martin to wait till you came so I wouldn't have to tell my little saga twice."

Before Celine could begin, a nurse entered. "The attending physician said you're free to go home. Follow the post-visit instructions in this summary," she said, handing Celine a few printed pages. "Take it easy the next few days and the Tylenol should take care of any pain. Call your own doctor if there are any complications."

Celine said simply, "Good."

The three of them moved to the waiting area and found a private corner where Martin moved a few chairs into a tight circle. A Cleveland policeman sat across the room reviewing papers in his lap.

Celine took a sip from her water bottle. "I was at the bar of Monty's Tavern talking to Skylark and Morgan about how happy I was that they were working on getting their GEDs. My ministry is pretty much getting to know the women and encouraging them to look beyond their present situation. I can't be too overtly religious or spiritual. That just wouldn't work. But I let them know I respect them and like them. And if I'm patient, sooner or later *they* want to talk about God and religion. I try to meet up with Skylark and Morgan, and about a dozen other women, two or three times a week at the bars where they hang out and at the fast-food places in the neighborhood. The Notre Dame Sisters provide a few things to give them, like tissue, hand creams, deodorant, shampoo—conveniences like that. They appreciate the kindness."

Amelia said, "Celine's been in this ministry for about four years now, Bishop. Her ministry is a little bit on the bleeding edge. Oh, maybe I shouldn't have said that."

Celine shook her head. "Spot on, Amelia!"

Martin nodded his agreement.

"I left Monty's at about four-thirty so I could get back to the apartment in time for vespers. I was at the door of my car when the girls'...*manager*...turned me around and started screaming at me. He grabbed my throat and pushed me against my car. I couldn't breathe. It was terrifying. He told me to leave his girls alone. He didn't want anyone talking to them about religion." Amelia took Celine's hand and held it. "Then he slapped me. Hard. Twice. The second time with the back of his hand. I think it was one of his rings that cut my cheek. His face was inches from mine. His eyes were glassy, and his teeth were a kind of grayish yellow. I was sure he was going to seriously hurt me, right there on the street. He has hurt a lot of them. 'Stay away from my girls,' he said again, and then he turned and stomped toward the back entrance to Monty's. It all happened so fast. Less than half a minute."

Both Bishop Martin and Sister Amelia seemed to hold their breath, then slowly shook their heads.

"I know very well who he is," said Celine. "His name is Howard. It's all in my statement."

Martin drove back to the cathedral rectory thinking about Skylark, Morgan, and the countless other young women and men caught in the dark, dangerous world of prostitution and sex trafficking in Cleveland. And he thought, too, of the priest who paid them for sex, whose darkness of soul he shuddered to imagine.

5

Bishop Bryn Martin took a first glance at his calendar for the day. His next appointment was with the superior of the Notre Dame Sisters of Chardon, Sister Amelia DiRosa. Terry Reeves, his chancellor and administrative assistant, had said the meeting was urgent. Sister Amelia, he knew, would be early for her two o'clock appointment. Sure enough, the nun was waiting when he opened his office door. Martin crossed the waiting area to her, extending his hand.

"Sister Amelia, welcome. Come in."

She stood and, without smiling, shook the hand of her bishop. "Thank you for seeing me, Bishop."

Martin was expecting a briefing on Sister Celine's progress since her attack. They sat near the windows of his corner office around a wood-veneered coffee table.

"Would you like coffee, Sister, or water?" Martin asked.

"I'm fine, Bishop," she said, her voice hinting at a bit of nerves. "But thank you."

"How is Sister Celine?"

"She's good. Back to her ministry with the street walkers. Some of the girls seem to have a new respect for her. Howard, however—the man who attacked her—was attacked himself. He told the ER doctors he fell down some stairs. He'll be okay but it looks like he broke the code: you don't mess with nuns."

Martin tilted his head and grinned. "Tell Sister Celine I said hello. Her work is important."

"I did, of course, want you to know that she's up and running, but there's another reason I needed to see you. But first I better explain a bit about my family. We're second-generation Italians. The DiRosa side of my family, who come from Naples, settled in the Newburgh section of Cleveland. My mother's a Scarano and her family lived in Rome before some of them immigrated to Pittsburgh and then came here."

Amelia hesitated before continuing. She appeared a bit uneasy to Martin. He decided to let her tell her story in her own time.

"The Scaranos who stayed in Rome were in the restaurant business. They have three or four restaurants. But that's not their principle source of income." Amelia took a deep breath. "I think you know where this is going, Bishop. Some of my mother's family who remained in Rome have ties to organized crime. And some, I can't say how many, have more than just ties. My uncle, Leonine Scarano, is now don of the Scarano family. They brag," Amelia blushed slightly, "that they're one of Rome's oldest Mafia families."

"Let me get you some water, Sister." Amelia didn't object.

When he returned, Amelia was standing at the window, gazing out at nothing in particular. They moved back to their chairs.

Amelia took a sip of water, then another. "Most of the Scaranos who came to the States settled, as I mentioned, in Cleveland. But I have cousins in Pittsburgh and Youngstown. To my knowledge, none of my relatives here are involved with the mob." Amelia smiled. "But if they were, it would be a bit awkward to tell me—the family nun—what they were up to." Martin nodded. "In fact, Bishop, one of my cousins just retired as police chief of Lyndhurst, and another cousin was mayor of Mayfield Heights." Amelia felt herself blush again, afraid she was sounding defensive about her family. "The Cleveland Scaranos have stayed in touch with the Rome Scaranos." Amelia took another sip of water and asked cautiously, "Bishop, are you planning to be in Rome anytime soon?"

Martin raised an eyebrow, "As a matter of fact, Sister, I'm going to Rome next week with Archbishop Cullen of Baltimore. He's going to be made a cardinal."

"I remember reading about the new batch of cardinals," Amelia said, somewhat distractedly.

Martin waited for her to explain her question. She seemed hesitant, so he filled the gap in the conversation, "Archbishop Cullen's a good friend. We got to know each other rather well when I was his auxiliary bishop. I'll be one of about thirty people in his official party." Amelia stirred uncomfortably. "Tell me why you asked?"

"My younger brother—he's an English teacher at Cleveland Central Catholic—received a text from one of our cousins in Rome. The message was, 'Your bishop and the Archbishop of Baltimore are in danger. Must be careful in Rome.' That was it. Nothing more."

Martin froze in his chair. Did Amelia know that one attempt had already been made on his life, not in Rome, but here in Cleveland?

Amelia broke the silence. "My brother called me yesterday as soon as he got the text. He thought I'd have a better chance of getting you to take the warning seriously than he would."

Martin's mind was racing, but he forced a smile. "Thank you for this information, Sister. I do take it seriously, and the next thing I am going to do is call Archbishop Cullen."

6

S ecret societies. They're quite fascinating." Professor Ian Landers scanned the faces of his students in his Secret Societies of Medieval Europe course at Johns Hopkins University. "How many of you belong to one?" No hands went up. "How about a fraternity or sorority?" About a third of the students raised their hand. "What do you think? Aren't fraternities and sororities secret societies?"

One of the women in the class raised her hand. "In light of your criteria for a secret society, I think they are. Their initiation rites are secret. That alone puts them into the category of a secret society."

A flurry of hands went up. The discussion was joined.

How did today's class go?" Dr. Nora Martin asked, leaning against the door frame of Ian Lander's office. Most of the faculty at John Hopkins, and many of their students, understood that they were an item.

"It went swimmingly," he said, still steeped in his Bloomsbury English after almost two decades in America. "In fact, we had a rather feisty discussion. When I inquired whether they thought their own fraternities and sororities were secret societies, I really got them going."

Nora grinned. "That's a good sign of engagement this early in the semester." She remained in the doorway. "I just arranged for my graduate assistant to cover my Thursday classes for our long weekend in Rome. How about you?"

"I'm good too. Four days in Rome. A rather tight window, but it should be fun. And guess what I just found out this morning. Archbishop Cullen is including my mother and her friend, Margaret Comiskey, in his official party! They're both astounded to be going to the installation of a cardinal."

"Given all that happened in Baltimore, they deserve to be invited to the party."

"They do. But it's still generous of Charles to include them. And we'll have time on the flight to Rome to toast their heroic deeds, which I'm sure we will relive high over the Atlantic."

"Yes, a toast to pederasts exposed, and murder schemes thwarted, and the two little old church ladies who made it all happen."

7

Ian Landers had been in his Johns Hopkins office since eight that morning. His lecture notes for his nine-thirty class sat in a purple file folder in front of him. He couldn't understand faculty colleagues who rushed directly from their cars to their classrooms. Some quiet time, that's what he always needed, a moment to establish a certain centeredness. Most often he felt a twinge of excitement, just a slight surge of energy, as class time approached. They were into the third week of the semester of his Secret Societies course, and he was satisfied that he'd gotten off to a good start.

By way of introduction he had begun with an overview of secret societies in ancient times, pointing out that they had remained an integral part of human endeavor from the dawn of civilization to the present day. And these early societies made a real impact. They dethroned kings, forged new dynasties, and transformed religious belief and practices. But what was their lasting power to draw people in? It was a question he had posed to his students during their first meeting. The course would help them answer that question, he had promised, and explore why secret societies have persisted in virtually every period of human history.

Landers turned off his desk lamp, put on his sports coat, gathered his notes, and headed to class.

"Today," Dr. Landers began, "we are moving from secret societies in ancient times to secret societies in medieval times, the main focus of our course. Be sure to review your notes on the mystery cults we discussed in our last class, the Eleusinian and Dionysian cults in particular. Any questions about them?"

Madison, a Black sophomore from Milwaukee, raised her hand. "It seems to me that what's secret about these societies is their secret rituals, rather than who belongs to them. Is that right?"

"There is an element of truth in what you say, Madison, but in many of these societies, keeping the members' identity secret was critically important." Landers paused for emphasis. "Secrecy is often linked to attempts to gain power. The other thing to keep in mind about these ancient societies is that they were grounded in mythology. In the Eleusinian cult, it was the myth of Demeter and Persephone. For the Dionysian cult, it was, of course, the myth of Dionysus, the Greek god of wine, fertility, and theater. This may be less true for the medieval societies, but the formation of secret societies, I would argue, is typically grounded in mythology. I'll say more about this later in the course, but there is a dimension in most secret societies of what I'll call a "mystery cult." Its members know something you don't. It's why we think of secret societies as esoteric."

Madison looked puzzled and took a different tack. "Dr. Landers, I want to go back to the discussion we had last week about whether fraternities and sororities are themselves secret societies."

"Yeah, me too," another voice burst out. The speaker was Jason, a senior from rural Kentucky. "I asked my frat brothers what they thought. We all agreed that our fraternity is not a secret society. We're just like-minded friends who like to party together and, we hope, will stay in touch after we graduate. Maybe help one another with our careers. We think of our initiation ritual as kind of a *private* thing rather than *secret*."

A number of hands went up. Julie, who belonged to one of the Catholic Worker communities of Baltimore, spoke out, "I don't buy your private versus secret distinction, Jason. Greek life is an elitist, exclusivist, quasi-secret part of college life that has outlived its time."

Her direct challenge put a charge in the air.

"Well, this provides a perfect segue into one of America's oldest secret societies," Landers said. "Any idea what that might be?"

Silence.

Landers continued, "The Phi Beta Kappa Society, many historians believe, is our first secret society. Others believe it was the Flat Hat Club, which surfaced in 1750. Thomas Jefferson was a member of that one. But for now let's focus on Phi Beta Kappa. It was founded in 1776 at the College of William and Mary in Williamsburg, Virginia. Its members embraced a motto, "Love of learning is a guide for life," in Greek—*Philosophia Biou Kybernētēs.* Candidates had to undergo an initiation ritual and learn symbols and verbal cues that could discreetly identify one Phi Beta Kappa to another." Landers moved to the whiteboard, picked up a red marker and wrote, "1832." "However, after Phi Beta Kappa took off its cloak of secrecy and became an open society, two Yale students in 1832 formed a new secret fraternity that is extant today, the Skull and Bones Society. Are you familiar with it?"

Most of the class nodded they were.

"Students need not apply," Landers said with a whimsical expression. "Every year fifteen Yale juniors are tapped for lifetime admittance into the society. You can guess what the criteria for the tap might be. Don't expect to find much diversity, but do expect to encounter a silent yet powerful network of well-connected sons of well-connected fathers who have strongly influenced our politics, government, business, and even the CIA—and continue to do so." He paused. "You may know that both presidential candidates for the 2004 election were Skull and Bones brothers—John Kerry and George W. Bush." Another pause. "Members refer to each other as 'Bonesmen.'" Landers didn't miss the grins on the faces of most of the men, and more than a few of the women, in the class.

8

Perugia, after dinner, in the archbishop's dining room

His Excellency, the Archbishop of Perugia, soon to be his Eminence, Cardinal Pietro Gonzaga Montaldo, sat like a medieval prince at the head of his candlelit and flower-bedecked table. The soft lighting failed to flatter the deep-set eyes and sharp aristocratic chin of the prelate, dressed in a tailored red cassock with a jeweled gold episcopal cross resting on his chest. To his right, the English priest and Anglican convert, Father Trace Dunmore, his master of ceremonies and the former chancellor of the Diocese of Cleveland. To his left, Simon Ashley, renegade faculty member from John Carroll University, now curator of the episcopal palace and the cathedral's extensive art collection. Though not acknowledged at the table, the debt Dunmore and Ashley owed to the archbishop rested on their shoulders like a yoke. Their sinecures—and their narrow escape from the American criminal justice system—were due entirely to the largesse of His Excellency.

"Of course, both of you," Montaldo said paternally, "will accompany me to Rome for the consistory."

Ashley gushed, "We are so grateful, Excellency, to be members of your official party."

Dunmore simply stared at Ashley, put off by his naked bootlicking.

"Alas," Montaldo sighed, "nothing goes quite as smoothly as one would like. Also to be installed into the college, as you know, is the Archbishop of Baltimore, Charles Cullen. I'm quite distressed at this situation, as you can well imagine."

Dunmore and Ashley nodded discreetly.

"Our Brotherhood of the Sacred Purple was making real progress in naming the right men as American bishops until poor Archbishop Wilfred Gunnison's vanity—and his imprudent behavior with boys—crashed down on him and our good work in the States."

Both listeners knew they had to endure this little lecture still again.

"Now Wilfred Gunnison is gone to his…reward…and my appointed leader of the American Brotherhood, Monsignor Aidan Kempe, is now the pastor of an insignificant parish in a very remote part of the Baltimore archdiocese." Montaldo took a deep breath. "I had no choice but to suppress the Brotherhood."

Ashley caught Dunmore's eye. *Only after ordering the assassination of Gunnison. And only for a short while. You wasted little time in establishing, with our essential help, the Sentinels of the Supreme Center.*

Montaldo sipped his dessert wine. "It is too bad that in the aftermath of Gunnison's folly the work of the Brotherhood came to the attention of Charles Cullen and his auxiliary bishop, Bryn Martin. Much worse, they discovered some of our financial channels, the lifeblood of our sacred mission." The archbishop went silent, glancing at both Dunmore and Ashley, who knew better than to interrupt the soliloquy. "Cullen and Martin," he said solemnly, "simply know too much about us. It is because of them we find ourselves in a very precarious position."

"I don't think Cullen and Martin really know that much," Dunmore offered tentatively. "They may know how Kempe added to his war chest, his Purple Purse, from the handful of pastors

41

he recruited into the Brotherhood, but I doubt they know much more."

Montaldo glared at Dunmore. "I'm afraid, Father Dunmore, that they know far more than you think. Both Cullen and Martin already know, or are likely to discover, that the Brotherhood of the Sacred Purple—and the Sentinels of the Supreme Center—can be traced to me." The archbishop sat up straight in his chair. "And that is not acceptable, not acceptable at all."

Ashley steamed where he sat. *The fact that the Brotherhood and the Sentinels can be traced to you, Pietro, is due to Kempe's bungling. Due to his arrogance. Unlike Kempe in Baltimore, we accomplished much in Cleveland.*

Dunmore, his eyes on his lap, sat still as a statue.

Montaldo reached for his water glass. After an uncomfortable silence, he said deliberately, "We have a chance to secure our sacred mission, to safeguard our secrecy, and strengthen our power. A chance given to us by providence. It is an opportunity that requires great boldness, great courage." The archbishop looked from Ashley to Dunmore and back again, a steely resolve in his eyes. "Neither Cullen nor Martin will leave Rome alive."

Later that night, Giorgio Grotti, fully clothed, lay on his bed in his modest suite in the episcopal palace of the Archbishop of Perugia. Worn out from the tedious drive up from Rome, Grotti felt frustrated. The consistory was only a week away. He had to begin as soon as possible to sketch out the specific steps he would have to take to get at his targets. But this was impossible without the intel Angelo Correa had agreed to get for him. Though frustrated and tired, Grotti had made some progress during his trip to Rome, but he had to trust that Correa could get the information he needed on Cullen and Martin. Only then could he begin the detailed planning of the operation. Getting close enough to strike at the two Americans was the first challenge. If possible, there would be no overt spilling of blood. Cullen would be poisoned. Perhaps the same for Martin. *But where, and when, by what means, and by whom?* The last question was one he had never had to ask before. He had always been the sole agent of Montaldo's attacks. Should he even consider Correa's suggestion to let Vittoria Massi make the hits? That possibility complicated everything. And what would Montaldo think about that? But he wouldn't have to know. And why would it matter? This would be Giorgio Grotti's last mission for the little prince. *Go slowly here,* he told himself. *Let's see if Vittoria Massi can come up with the right potion for the job.* He would have to meet her, of course, before deciding. Grotti wondered if she was as sexy as Angelo implied, and whether his bankroll might entitle him to some special benefits. He'd give Correa a call in the morning.

He kicked off his shoes and turned out the light, too exhausted to even undress.

9

Bishop Bryn Martin's first instinct after Sister Amelia left his office was to call Charles Cullen. But he didn't. He sat at his desk processing what he had just heard from the superior of the Sisters of Notre Dame of Chardon. Why not let the man enjoy these few days of joyful anticipation with his Catholic Center staff and the Catholics of Baltimore? To bask in the positive coverage he was getting from the friends in the media he had come to cultivate. This was a big deal for Catholic Baltimore. It had been decades since the first Catholic diocese in the country had been able to claim a cardinal archbishop.

But he knew the warning required immediate action. Instead of calling Cullen, he dialed Terry Reeves, his chancellor and administrative assistant.

"Terry, Do you remember Duane Moore and George Havel?" A retired FBI agent and a retired CIA agent respectively, the two men had become friends of the bishop's while trying to thwart an assassination attempt against retired Archbishop Wilfred Gunnison in Baltimore. Martin had called on them for help once again during a series of murders of women priests in Cleveland.

"Those law enforcement guys, sure," Reeves said.

"Do you still have contact information?"

"If not, I'll get it."

"Please arrange a conference call with them as soon as you can."

There was a moment of silence on the line before Reeves asked, "Is there something I need to know about?"

Martin mulled that over. "No need yet," he said. "It may be nothing."

Two hours later, Reeves had both Havel and Moore on the phone.

"Once again, guys, I need your help," Martin said after a brief catch up.

"Whatever we can do, Bishop."

"Amen."

"I just met with Sister Amelia DiRosa, the president, the mother superior, of the Sisters of Notre Dame. She's Italian, third generation, with family ties back in Italy. Her mother's maiden name is Scarano. The Scaranos, she informed me, are one of Rome's oldest Mafia families. The Cleveland Scaranos, I understand, are pretty far removed from organized crime, but they stay in touch with their cousins in Italy. Someone in the Scarano family sent a text message to her brother here in Cleveland that said: 'Your bishop and the Archbishop of Baltimore are in danger. Must be careful in Rome.'"

Both Havel and Moore exhaled audibly but neither spoke.

"Archbishop Cullen has invited me to accompany him to Rome for the consistory that will make him a cardinal. I'm to fly to Rome with his official party next week."

"Would you like us to come?" Moore broke in.

"No, I don't think so. I believe we'll have sufficient protection from Vatican and Italian authorities."

Havel added, "You'll need to be very careful, especially in light of the intrigue surrounding Archbishop Gunnison's death and all that happened in Cleveland last year."

Martin smiled at George Havel's discretion. Like Martin, Havel and Moore both believed that Cullen's predecessor had not taken his own life, as the authorities had pronounced, but had been murdered. And they also suspected that the murderer was working for a secret society of archconservative Vatican clergy.

"Here's how you two can help. Can you find out what your respective agencies have on the Scarano family? I'd like to know if they can be linked to the Vatican Bank, or to any Vatican officials." Martin, assuming their cooperation, didn't wait for a response. "What I'm going to ask now is especially delicate. Can you find out if your agencies have a file on one Pietro Gonzaga Montaldo, recently appointed Archbishop of Perugia. He is to be made a cardinal at the same consistory as Archbishop Cullen."

"Anything else on your Christmas list, Bishop?" Moore said with a chuckle.

"I'm afraid there is one more thing. You two will remember that the assassin who almost murdered Margaret Comiskey got into her house by identifying himself as 'Monsignor Giancarlo Foscari.' He showed her Vatican credentials that appeared authentic. I doubt that's his real name, but he may have traveled with a Vatican passport using that name. Vatican passports aren't that common. See if Homeland Security has any record of a Giancarlo Foscari. I expect this Foscari is the mysterious figure we got a glimpse of at Archbishop Gunnison's Jubilee Mass."

Martin held his breath. *Best not tell them I suspect it was Foscari who killed Fergus Mann in my place.*

Moore said tentatively, "I think I know who to call."

I'll make some discreet calls too," Havel said. "We all know how careful we need to be if we go hunting for confidential information about a future cardinal of the Catholic Church."

"Thank you, George," Martin said softly. "I realize I'm asking a lot. If either of you get any resistance, of course, back off. But if you make any headway, look for a connection between Pietro Montaldo and the major financiers and bankers of Rome. He's sitting on huge sums of money, money he's using to support a network of secret societies committed—at any cost—to restoring the church to its glory days before Vatican II. And look for a connection between Montaldo and the Scarano family. You both have my cell number. Call, don't text." Martin thought for a moment and added, "I'd love to know how the Scarano family came to hear that Archbishop Cullen and I might be in danger when we're in Rome."

His mind spinning, Bryn Martin hung up the phone, rose from his desk, and paced around his Catholic Center office. What did all this mean? How much danger, if any, were he and Charles really in? Should they even consider canceling the trip altogether? Maybe it was a false alarm. Thank God for George Havel and Duane Moore.

Bryn Martin left his office and headed for the kitchenette area on the sixth floor of the Catholic Center. A few minutes later, with a mug of black coffee in hand, he stood at the windows of his office overlooking East Ninth Street. The movement of cars and pedestrians six floors below distracted him for a moment. He reviewed what he knew about the two secret societies that had surfaced, one in Baltimore, another in Cleveland. The new Archbishop of Perugia, it seemed, was the key to it all. It was Ian Landers who first tipped him off to Pietro Montaldo as the likely grand master of both the Brotherhood of the Sacred Purple and the Sentinels of the Supreme Center. Ian got the information from an Oxford colleague, a Dominican priest, Father Tom Hathaway, now teaching at the Angelicum, the Dominican Pontifical University in Rome. Montaldo was widely known to be an archconservative with a passionate commitment to restoring the church to its pre-Vatican II clarity and the clergy to the position of power he deemed rightful. But there were also whispered conversations over cocktails that Montaldo maintained a sophisticated network of secret societies in Europe and North America committed to his "reform of the reform" crusade. Thanks to Ian's Dominican friend, Martin was reasonably sure the mysterious M that he first heard of when he was Cullen's auxiliary was this Archbishop Montaldo. And it was Margaret Comiskey, then secretary to Monsignor Aidan Kempe, the chancellor of the Archdiocese of Baltimore, who had first come across the enigmatic M. If Montaldo was the grand master of the Brotherhood, Kempe must be his local deputy. When Cullen discovered Kempe's betrayal, he removed him as chancellor and exiled him to a parish far from the heart of the archdiocese. While the Brotherhood of the Sacred Purple seemed to soon disappear, its offspring, the Sentinels of the Sacred Purple, had surfaced in Martin's own Cleveland diocese and could still be operating secretly right before his eyes. The thought left him cold...and scared.

Leaving his Catholic Center office, Martin walked across East Ninth Street to the cathedral rectory. It was time to pack for his trip to Rome.

10

Angelo Correa and Giorgio Grotti sat alone at the end of the bar close to the kitchen in the Ristorante Carlo. They could hear the muffled voices of the chef's staff and the annoying clatter of pots and pans.

Correa smiled, "Just so you know, Giorgio, the don had some misgivings about the family cooperating with one of Montaldo's people. But I got the nod. 'Proceed with caution,' he said. Overall, it might be good for business. But Leo Scarano really doesn't like Montaldo. He knows he's a snake, even if we have to work with him." Angelo wagged a finger at Grotti. "You might be shocked at some of the operations His Excellency is involved in."

Grotti wondered what he was hinting at. Montaldo's gay capers perhaps. But he didn't want to appear completely in the dark. "So what have you found out?" he asked lamely.

"This is a rather large batch of new cardinals, fifteen, as you know. Twelve will be coming to Rome for the consistory. Three are either too old to travel or can't come for political reasons. Cullen's party, including Bishop Martin, are staying at the Hotel Raphael on Largo Febo. A nice enough place. He's reserved a few dozen rooms, two whole floors." Correa reached into the breast pocket of his jacket and pulled out a folded paper and slid it over to Grotti. "Here's a list of his guests as of yesterday."

Cullen was at the top of the list, followed by Martin. Grotti, with a finger pressed to the paper, moved down the list: Dr. Nora Martin, Dr. Ian Landers, Ella Landers, and a long list of names he didn't recognize. Grotti stopped suddenly at the name Margaret Comiskey. His spine stiffened as a chill ran through his body. He remembered being in this woman's Baltimore home, posing as Monsignor Giancarlo Foscari. Montaldo had ordered him to eliminate her but, by the grace of God, called off the assassination just seconds before he would have strangled the life from her. If he hadn't had his cell phone with him, Comiskey would be with the saints right now. But she was very much alive, it seemed, and soon to be in Rome. This Margaret Comiskey could identify him, and perhaps have him charged with attempted murder.

"You okay, Giorgio? You look surprised."

"There's a name on this list I didn't expect to see. It complicates the whole operation." Grotti looked again at the list of names, then sideways at Angelo and said, with a slight tremor in his voice, "I need to meet Vittoria Massi as soon as possible."

11

Archbishop Charles Cullen had managed to get all of the thirty-two members of his official party into the United Club near their gate in Terminal C of Newark's International Airport. And his longtime friends and benefactors of the archdiocese, Marcus and Florence Merriman, to his surprise, had upgraded much of Cullen's inner circle to business class for the nine-hour flight to Rome's Fiumicino Airport. Cullen sat with the Merrimans, the three of them sipping champagne, as he again thanked them for their generosity. "What a wonderful thing to do," Cullen said, adding that they would be guests of the archdiocese at the Hotel Raphael.

Marcus took his wife's hand. "Florence and I are happy to help make this a special celebration, especially after all you have been through recently."

Florence, dressed casually in a dark-blue running suit, smiled. "Both Marcus and I are so grateful to be included in your official party, Charles. This will be truly..." her eyes widened... "an affair to remember."

Martin stood across the room talking to a few of the chancery priests; all seemed thrilled and proud that their boss was about to bring a cardinal's red hat back to Baltimore. Catching the archbishop's eye, Martin walked across the room.

51

"Please excuse me," Martin said after greeting Marcus and Florence, "but I need a quick word with Charles before we go." The two men moved to a quiet corner of the United Club and sank into comfortable chairs placed side by side.

Cullen's round Irish face revealed only a hint of apprehension. "What is it, Bryn?"

"Just before I left Cleveland," Martin began deliberately, "the superior of one of our religious congregations asked to see me. Her name is Sister Amelia DiRosa. I don't know her well, but I have reason to respect her greatly. Her grandparents immigrated to the States from Italy and her mother's side of the family, the Scaranos, have relatives who are entrenched Mafia in Rome. How, I don't know, but somehow, the Scarano family heard that we might be in danger during the consistory. Someone in the family sent a message—a warning—through a family member in Cleveland."

The color drained from Cullen's cheeks.

"The message sent by text was short. 'Your bishop and the Archbishop of Baltimore are in danger. Must be careful in Rome.'"

Cullen slouched in his chair, the air sucked out of him. He reached into his coat pocket and patted at two small plastic bottles, meds for his high blood pressure and AFib. "What do you make of it, Bryn?"

"I'm not really sure. On the one hand it's a vague message, without context, from a Mafia family in Rome. But why send such a warning? Do we have a friend in the Scarano family? How are they involved? And after all that's happened, I am certain we need to take this as a serious threat. You remember George Havel and Duane Moore, who helped us on the Archbishop Gunnison matter? I've got them working on this."

Cullen tilted his head and leaned in close to Martin. "Thanks for that, Bryn. This secret brotherhood of the super orthodox that we had to deal with in Baltimore and your experience with a similar secret society…what did they call themselves?"

"The Sentinels of the Supreme Center," Martin whispered.

"These people," Cullen continued, "really scare me."

"Me too," Martin said. "What we know of them…" Martin closed his eyes. "…What we know of their readiness to assassinate their enemies…" Again he stopped. In the silence that followed, Martin thought of the murder of Archbishop Gunnison, the attempt on the life of Margaret Comiskey, the murder of two Catholic women priests in Cleveland, and the mistaken-identity murder of a retired policeman—himself a killer—who had been killed in Martin's stead.

"You're right, of course, Bryn, we need to be on guard." An ironic smile crossed Cullen's face as he shook his head. "Nothing is ever easy, is it? Even an honor from the pope."

Martin looked up to catch the concerned gaze of Florence Merriman. She knew, he could tell, that the conversation between her two friends had taken a serious bent. She leaned over and whispered something to her husband. But someone else caught Martin's eye. Walking into the United Club in full clerical garb was Monsignor Aidan Kempe, followed by his two closest priest friends, Thomas Fenton and Herman Volker. Martin bit his tongue. *They must be on the same flight to Rome. This is going to be an awkward nine hours.*

Martin elbowed the archbishop, "Look who's here."

Cullen took a deep breath and exhaled a sigh of exasperation. "Of course. Why am I surprised?"

Martin scanned the crowded United Club looking for Margaret Comiskey. She apparently hadn't seen Kempe yet, but it would be just a matter of time. She sat with her old friend, Ella Landers, Ian's mother. Seated across from them were Martin's sister Nora, and Ian. No animated conversation, just the slightly anxious pre-flight chatter of travelers, eased by sparkling glasses of champagne. Martin sensed their anticipation. The consistory celebration was just one part of the excursion. The business-class flight, the dinners in some of Rome's best restaurants, a few days of free time in one of the world's most beautiful cities, the consistory itself, the Mass with the pope the next day....

But for Archbishop Charles Cullen and Bishop Bryn Martin, the party was already over.

12

Thirty-three thousand feet over the Atlantic

Bryn Martin was frustrated. The business-class seats were certainly comfortable, really beds in disguise, with each seat set in a low-walled cocoon of privacy. Ideal for the traveler's privacy and comfort, but not at all designed for easy conversation. And he and Charles needed to talk...and talk privately. Martin stood at his seat and studied the layout of the spacious business class compartment. About sixty seats, fifteen rows with four across in most of the rows—two in the center of the cabin and one at each window. Martin, Cullen, Nora, and Ian were in seats clustered close to one another, but in an area not at all suited for private conversation. Martin stood and tried to look disinterested as he cast his eye around the cabin. Aidan Kempe and his friends were on the opposite side of the plane. *Thank God for that.* Kempe and Cullen had avoided each other in the United Club before the boarding call for their flight. But sooner or later...

Margaret Comiskey and Ian's mother, Ella, were seated midway through the section. Martin couldn't tell if Margaret knew yet that her former boss, the man whose downfall she had helped engineer, Monsignor Aidan Kempe, was settling in just four rows ahead of her.

Finally, the plane began creeping back from the gate. Forty-

55

five minutes later, just out over the Atlantic, a bit of static on the PA system signaled a message from the flight deck. "Welcome aboard United Flight 27 to Rome's Fiumicino Airport. I'm Captain Brad Cauley, assisted by one of United Airline's veteran, international crews. Our cruising altitude will be 33,000 feet and we expect a smooth flight, with the wind at our backs. Our scheduled flight time is eight hours and ten minutes. It's 4,293 air miles, 6,909 kilometers, and 3,730 nautical miles to Rome." He offered a friendly chuckle, then said, "Remember to keep your seat belts fastened even when the seat belt sign is off. Thanks for flying United. Sit back and enjoy the flight."

A grim smile crossed Martin's face. There was absolutely no chance he would enjoy this flight. Just before boarding, he had briefed his sister and Ian about the cryptic warning from Rome. Cullen had agreed with him that, at least for the time being, Margaret Comiskey should not be told about it. Perhaps when they were settled in Rome, but not now. His plan was to gather after the meal was served and most of the business-class cabin was bedded down to sleep away the long hours ahead. Then he, Cullen, Nora, and Ian would find a place to huddle, maybe at the self-serve bar in the middle of the cabin. Even that was iffy. They might not have the bar to themselves. Perhaps Nora and Ian could hunker down against the bulkhead in front of Charles' seat and he could squat in the aisle. *Enough for now.*

Martin sat back down and sipped the glass of malbec on the shelf to his left. He should be hungry, but the adrenaline racing through him had damped his appetite. But this would be a long night and he had to eat something. Without much interest, he picked up the menu and chose the first thing that caught his eye. No dessert...just plenty of black coffee.

Two hours later, with the cabin lights dimmed, Martin stood at the bar of the business-class cabin with Cullen, Nora, and Ian. They stood shoulder to shoulder in a tight semi-circle speaking softly, almost whispering.

Nora said, "We have to believe this warning must be linked, however indirectly, to the groups we've encountered already. We know all too well that their kind of fanaticism can be deadly."

"As soon as we land," Martin said, "I'm going to alert the Vatican police, the Carabinieri, and the Polizia di Stato. Let's hope they'll give us the security we need."

"The consistory must go forward with as few distractions as possible," Cullen insisted. "Not only the liturgies in St. Peter's, but the dinners and receptions too."

The other three nodded.

"Going through customs," Ian proposed, "Charles and Bryn should be somewhat separated but never alone, never standing by themselves. Charles, I'll be at your elbow until we get on the bus taking us to our hotel. Nora, you should stay close to Bryn. Getting safely on the bus and to our hotel is the first objective. And Bryn," Ian hesitated… "you might want to wait until we are at the hotel before you contact the authorities."

"Yes, passport control, baggage, customs, boarding the bus… let's take care of that first," Martin agreed.

Cullen shifted his weight. "Bryn, I'm feeling uneasy about contacting the Carabinieri and the State Police. I'd rather you first contact the Vatican police and see what they advise. Let our own security experts decide if the others should be involved. The last thing we want is a media circus. The Vatican gendarmes will be careful about that. And they'll know if the Swiss Guard should be in the loop."

"Makes sense," Martin said softly.

A flight attendant passed by. "Is everything all right? This looks like a pretty serious conversation," she said lightly as she moved on to the premium-economy section of the plane.

No sooner had the flight attendant gone by than a passenger in a seat some rows away stood up awkwardly and moved with tentative steps toward the restrooms across the aisle from the bar. Monsignor Aidan Kempe, still in his coat and collar, avoided eye contact with Cullen and his entourage as he slipped into one of the cabins. "Excuse me," Martin said suddenly, "I'll be back in a minute." He disappeared into the back of the plane.

Five minutes later he was back at the bar. "This spot really isn't working. There are a few empty rows in the very back of the plane. Follow me." They moved in single file down the starboard aisle of the plane and seated themselves in the last of several empty rows. The flight attendant they had just seen gave them a quizzical look as they passed but simply shrugged.

"This is very interesting," Nora resumed, with a touch of irony. "Monsignor Kempe, we have to assume, is going to the consistory where you are going to get your red hat, Charles."

"He's going," Ian corrected, "to witness the installation of M to the College of Cardinals. It's pretty clear that the mysterious M of the Brotherhood of the Sacred Purple is Pietro Gonzaga Montaldo. And Aidan Kempe, his loyal knight, isn't going to miss this party."

Martin looked at Ian. "Your friend at the Angelicum knew what he was talking about."

"The pieces are falling into place. My other Oxford colleagues, Father Trace Dunmore and Simon Ashley, are also part of Montaldo's mission to save the church from liberals. Don't be surprised when they show up at the consistory too. If my source is right, both are part of Montaldo's household in Perugia. They'll be there."

"Ian," Nora said, "You could very easily make this…this saga of the Brotherhood of the Sacred Purple and the Sentinels of the Supreme Center a kind of epilogue to your course on the Secret

Societies of the Middle Ages."

"You're reading my mind."

"Let me talk this out," Cullen said suddenly. "Tell me if I'm missing something."

"Go ahead," Nora whispered.

"My predecessor, Wilfred Gunnison, was part of this secret fraternity, the Brotherhood of the Sacred Purple. And so was my chancellor, Aidan Kempe, along with a half dozen or so other priests. Tom Fenton and Herm Volker for sure. And it looks like they're taking orders from a bishop in Rome known as M, who we now are sure is Pietro Montaldo. Moreover, this brotherhood is willing to go to any lengths to restore the Catholic Church to their calcified vision of it." Cullen thought for a second. "Then this well-funded, tightly knit Brotherhood seems to just disappear, and a curiously similar cell, now including at least one layman, surfaces in Cleveland—The Sentinels of the Supreme Center. And here again, Montaldo's fingerprints seem to be all over the murder of two irregularly ordained Roman Catholic women."

"Let's not forget Monsignor Giancarlo Foscari. We may encounter him again." Martin's voice trailed off. He was too tired to think, his blue eyes taking on a gray cast. "If it's okay with you, Charles, let's meet in your suite at the Raphael an hour after we get to our rooms."

"Before we try to get some sleep," Nora said looking kindly at Cullen, "I think you missed the real elephant in the sanctuary. By what unholy instrument did a man like Montaldo climb up the ecclesial ladder from bishop to archbishop to cardinal of the Roman Catholic Church?"

13

Rome, midday

There's a message for you, Bishop Martin," the hotel clerk announced with enthusiasm, as if it had come directly from the highest levels of the Holy See. Martin thought at first that it might be from George Havel or Duane Moore. The message was sealed inside a small off-white envelope. "Bishop Bryn Martin" was printed in block letters with "Hotel Raphael" underneath his name. Martin, thinking better of opening the letter in the lobby, slipped it into the side pocket of his suitcoat and completed the registration process. Keycard in hand, he pulled his roller bag to the elevators. The meeting he had called in Cullen's suite for an hour after their arrival was clearly a bad idea. He had slept no more than two hours on the plane. Finally in his room, Martin fought the temptation to flop onto the bed. Instead, he moved to the chair at the small desk and turned on the lamp. He laid the letter on the desk and stared at it. Perhaps he should call the Vatican police before opening it. Cautiously, he slit the envelope open, handling it as if it were a piece of evidence. He slid out a single sheet of paper with a handwritten message.

Be at the alleyway next to the Caffè Sant'Eustachio,
behind the Pantheon, at 9:00 tonight. Come alone.
You have nothing to fear.
Careful in Rome

Martin read the message again…and then again. "Careful in Rome" was an obvious reference to the warning that Sister Amelia had delivered. So why did he feel a cold nugget of fear rising in his chest. Instinctively, he reached for the phone on the desk.

"Front desk. How can I help you?"

"This is Bishop Martin, please connect me with the Vatican police."

An hour later, Martin strode through the open door into the suite of Archbishop Cullen. Not only did he find Cullen, Nora, and Ian there, but the Inspector General of the Pontifical Gendarmerie as well.

"Bishop Martin, I'm Inspector General Tosco. I came as soon as I got your message," he said.

"I am very aware of who you are, sir." Martin had visited the Pontifical Gendarmerie's web site before leaving Cleveland. He learned that Lorenzo Tosco had been appointed by the pope as chief of the Vatican's police force three years earlier. He was an expert in cybersecurity and headed a small but well-trained corps of 140 men. To Martin's surprise, a few dozen were trained as a special ops corps—the GIR, the Rapid Intervention Group. So while the Gendarmerie were a relatively small force, they apparently were a competent and technologically sophisticated organization. "Thank you for coming so quickly after my call, Inspector."

Tosco nodded. "Let's sit down, shall we," he said in only slightly accented English. "Before you arrived, Archbishop Cullen told me of the message you received, allegedly from a member of the Scarano family of Rome." He consulted his notebook, "'Your bishop and the Archbishop of Baltimore are in danger. Must be careful in Rome.' Tell me, Bishop Martin, what do you make of this?"

Martin looked at Nora, Ian, and Cullen as if to say, *Sorry to put you through this.* "The four of us previously stumbled onto two secret groups of ultraconservative, traditionalist Catholics who are passionately committed to restoring the church's pre-Vatican II regal supremacy—by any means, even violence, if necessary. It appears these groups, whose leader we believe is a highly placed Vatican prelate, are afraid that Archbishop Cullen and I know too much about their finances, structure, and methods. I believe they see the two of us as a serious threat to their mission. A member of my staff at the chancery in Baltimore, Margaret Comiskey, actually survived an aborted attempt on her life because she had come to know too much about one of the groups. She has joined us here in Rome for the consistory. She is the only eyewitness to an actual crime, and I'm afraid she might be in danger as well."

"And the identity of this Vatican prelate?" Tosco said. The party from Baltimore exchanged uncomfortable looks. Martin lifted his arms towards the archbishop in a gesture to put him center stage.

"His identity is mere conjecture at this point," Cullen said. "We would not want to make an accusation that might not be true."

"Especially against a man so highly placed," Ian said.

"And what do you make of the warning?" Lorenzo pressed.

"Archbishop Cullen and I apparently have a friend in the Scarano family. What's puzzling to me is how they would have

62

discovered a plot against us? And why did they alert us?"

Tosco rested his note pad on his knee. "This might not ease your anxiety, but threats against Vatican prelates often come to our attention. Most of them remain idle threats. In your case, however," Lorenzo looked to Cullen and Martin, "we have not a threat, but a warning."

"Inspector General," Nora said with a worried look, "If the warning is connected to the Brotherhood of the Sacred Purple or the Sentinels of the Supreme Center, I believe we need to be very careful. These groups have both killed before."

Tosco looked straight at Nora and said evenly, "Dr. Martin, I will immediately notify the Carabinieri of the warning you have received and alert the captain of the Swiss Guard. The Carabinieri and the Vatican Gendarmerie, by the way, have a good working relationship. They employ a skilled intelligence network that has often been helpful in situations like this." Tosco hesitated before adding, "I see no need at this time to inform the Polizia di Stato."

Martin wanted to ask why, but thought better of it.

As if reading each other's minds, Ian Landers and Nora moved to the suite's tall windows and closed the drapes.

The Inspector General nodded his approval. "I am going to assign two gendarmes to pay special attention to you, Archbishop Cullen, and to you, Bishop Martin. They will not be in uniform nor will they be intrusive, but they will be close by. Correct me if I'm mistaken, Archbishop, but it's my understanding that the Office of Pontifical Ceremonies assigns a secretary who serves as an aide to each of the new cardinals for the consistory itself, for the Mass with the pope, and for the individual receptions, the *visite di cortesia*."

Cullen smiled, "Yes. And new cardinals each have a church in Rome put under their honorary care and protection. The Church of St. Lucretia has been assigned to me. That secretary will also assist me when I take titular possession there."

Tosco raised his eyebrows, "I will make sure that assistant, appropriately vested, will be one of my men."

This is getting complicated, Cullen thought. But Bryn seemed to like the idea, as did Nora and Ian.

"What I need now, Archbishop, is an hour-by-hour schedule for your stay in Rome. I'm assuming Bishop Martin will be with you at the various ceremonies and the like."

But with a few noted exceptions, Martin said to himself.

"Well, tonight I'm hosting a simple meal at a restaurant within walking distance of the hotel for my friends and family," Cullen said. "Tomorrow morning is unscheduled. Many will be resting; some might do some shopping or sightseeing. The consistory itself is at three o'clock in St. Peter's Basilica, followed by the *visite di cortesia* from six to eight. Each new cardinal is assigned a designated area in the Papal Palace or the Aula Paolo VI for friends, family, and well-wishers. An official photographer will be on hand and my secretary will distribute memento cards."

Cullen felt a tad embarrassed at all the pomp surrounding his elevation.

"Archbishop Cullen..." Ian quickly caught his mistake... "*Cardinal* Cullen might be especially vulnerable at his reception. Don't you think, Inspector?"

"Yes, that's true, Dr. Landers," Tosco replied. "But we need to think that every time the archbishop and bishop are out of their rooms they are vulnerable. You must both be sure you know who is at your door before opening it at any hour. I'm going to request that a plainclothes carabiniere be assigned to the lobby of the Raphael."

"The next day, Sunday," Cullen resumed reviewing his *horarium*, "we concelebrate a Mass with the pope and receive the cardinal's ring from him. Then the new cardinals give the kiss of peace to all the members of the college who are present." Cullen smiled. "I've been told this can take quite some time." He caught himself. "I'm sorry, Inspector General, perhaps you don't need these particulars." His cheeks flushed with embarrassment. "I expect you may know them better than I." The archbishop felt absolved by Tosco's bemused expression. "Sunday evening, I'm hosting a dinner for my friends and the Baltimore Catholic Center staff who were able to make the trip. That's at seven o'clock, at La Compana."

"A good choice," Tosco said. "A modest restaurant, really good food, perhaps Rome's oldest restaurant. Can you add me to your guest list for the dinner there? I would like to be in the dining room, at a table fairly close to yours."

"Of course," Cullen responded.

Martin nodded and returned to their timeline. "Monday is unscheduled. Time for the Baltimore party to see a bit of Rome. We're scheduled to leave the Raphael for the airport Tuesday morning at eight," Martin said.

"It's a long, packed weekend, Inspector General," Cullen said, looking exhausted already.

Tosco looked at his note pad then directly at Cullen. "And your transportation while in Rome? I want to have you and Bishop Martin covered as you move about the city."

"We have rented two motor coaches that can get my whole party around," Cullen replied.

Tosco said, "We'll have people moving with you as much as we can."

"One more thing I should mention," Cullen added, "sometime this afternoon I need to go to a clergy vestment store, Mancinelli Clero, to pick up my cardinal's regalia for the consistory. They've had my measurements on file and promised everything would be ready today."

"I'll send a car for you, Archbishop. What time would you like to be picked up?"

"Three o'clock or so. Mancinelli is on Borgo Pio."

"Yes, I know it," Tosco smiled as he rose to leave.

"Would you please sit another moment, Inspector General? There's something else," Martin said somewhat ominously. Tosco moved back to his chair. "There was a strange message for me at the registration desk when I checked in." He glanced at Cullen as he drew the envelope from his coat pocket. Nora and Ian slid to the edge of their chairs.

"I'd like you to hear it."

Martin opened the envelope and took out the small single sheet and read it. " 'Be at the alleyway next to the Café Sant'Eustachio, behind the Pantheon, at 9:00 tonight. Come alone. You have nothing to fear.' It's signed, 'Careful in Rome.' The sender has to be the person who sent the text message to me before I left Cleveland. It included that exact phrase."

Nora looked from her brother to Tosco. Was Bryn seriously thinking of meeting with this stranger? Could Montaldo be behind this? Did Bryn really have nothing to fear? "I don't like this at all, Bryn," she said. "Sure, it looks like a message from the person who sent you the warning. But the 'come alone' part scares me."

Cullen turned to the Inspector General. "What do you make of this?"

"May I see the note, Bishop?" Martin passed the message to Tosco.

"The Café Sant'Eustachio is a popular coffee shop. It will be busy at that time of the evening. I think you will be okay if you want to meet this person. And the alleyway next to the coffee shop…it's a very narrow street, yes, but not exactly a dark alley."

"I do want to meet this person," Martin said emphatically. "I'll be at the Café Sant'Eustachio at nine, but I'd appreciate having you, Inspector General, or one of your gendarmes close by… and not in uniform."

"You won't see me or the men I will have in the vicinity of the café. Nor will the person you will be meeting see us," Tosco promised.

14

Charles Cullen, too exhausted to risk stretching out on his bed, felt foolish standing at his hotel-room window looking out at nothing in particular. Two sharp knocks on the door broke his reverie. Cullen crossed the room and stood at the door, not sure what to do. Again, two staccato knocks.

"Who is it?"

"Inspector General Tosco sent me. I'm with the Vatican Gendarmerie."

Cullen looked at his watch. Five after three. He took a deep breath, checked that the swing bar door guard was set in the locked position, and opened the door a few inches.

A rather tall man in a business suit held up his Vatican credentials. The name on the card read "Paolo Corsi."

"I'm here to take you to Mancinelli, Archbishop."

Cullen hesitated then said, "I'll be right with you." He put on his black suit coat, made sure he had his wallet and key card, confirmed that the door locked behind him, and followed Corsi to the elevator.

Once outside, Corsi opened the right rear passenger door to a dark-gray Audi and Cullen clambered in. Corsi took the driver's seat, started the car, and swerved abruptly into heavy Roman traffic. *Too fast*, Cullen thought. "Do you have the address?" He was about to say, "Borgo Pio," when he caught Corsi's nod in the rearview mirror.

Cullen leaned back in the seat and tried to relax. This certainly was no official police vehicle. Leather seats and no sign of a radio.

Corsi glanced into the mirror and said without a smile, "Congratulations, Archbishop. Tomorrow you'll be a cardinal." Cullen thought for an instant he was going to say, "Congratulations, Archbishop. Tomorrow you'll be dead."

Corsi adjusted the rearview mirror with a glance behind them, then looked to the left side mirror. "Fasten your seatbelt, Archbishop. We're being followed," he said speeding ahead even faster. A few minutes later Cullen heard his driver mutter to himself, "He's good! I can't shake him." Cardinals wear red robes, Cullen remembered, because they are expected to be prepared to shed their blood to guard the unity of the church and the well-being of the pope. He clasped the grab handle above the door with his right hand, his stomach churning in a hard knot.

Corsi, barely braking, made sharp turn after sharp turn, driving furiously down narrow streets and suddenly onto a wide boulevard. After a final cut he skidded to a stop in a parking lot.

"Stay in the car!" he barked.

Corsi got out and turned toward the pursuing vehicle.

Cullen looked through the rear window as his protector approached the car in angry strides. He flashed his credentials. It sounded like the two drivers were cursing at each other. The confrontation ended abruptly as Corsi threw his arms up in the air and waved the pursuing auto back into the street. With what seemed like a smile, he walked back to the Audi.

"You Americans, Excellency," he said, trying to keep from laughing. "You were being followed by two reporters covering your elevation to the cardinalate. They work for the *Baltimore Sun*. Wanted to know where you were going. I expect they'll be tailing you for the next two days."

Relieved, Cullen collapsed back in his seat and looked up at the building above him. Corsi had driven into the parking lot of a district station of the Carabinieri. He smiled in spite of himself. *I guess the whole thing is rather comical.*

"I better get you to Mancinelli," Corsi said, starting the car.

Twenty minutes later, with his composure somewhat restored, Archbishop Cullen walked into Mancinelli with his bodyguard leading the way. He knew a little of the shop's history, which had driven his decision to order his episcopal robes there. The better-known clerical vestment and clothier to Vatican prelates was Gammarelli, established in the late eighteenth century. But recent popes had turned to the relative newcomer, Raniero Mancinelli, who catered to the tastes of prelates looking for perhaps less ostentatious vestments and clerical garb. Cullen proudly counted himself among those churchmen. But simplified or not, cardinals still costumed up like medieval princes. And for some, the more lace the better.

"Your robes are ready, Archbishop," the tailor said. "Please, if you would try on the cardinal's cassock. We might have to make some adjustments. We want you to look perfect."

Forty-five minutes later, with Paolo Corsi helping to carry three packed garment bags to the car, Cullen left the shop bearing his scarlet biretta and zucchetto in a separate plastic bag. Parked directly behind the Audi was the car that had followed him from the hotel. Cullen, his face flushed, smiled wanly at its occupants.

15

Exhausted as much by the stress of his trip to the tailor as his lingering jetlag, Cullen forged on to the light supper he had arranged for his official party. The five-minute walk to the Mater Terrae restaurant felt like a climb up five flights of stairs. His idea had been to have a light supper with his friends and retreat to his room early to be ready for the big day to follow.

Cullen had ordered for the entire party—bruschetta, Italian wedding soup, and linguine with clam sauce. After enjoying the meal and a few glasses of house wine, he seemed to recoup a bit of his energy. He was happy to see his Baltimore friends, in spite of their fatigue, enjoying themselves in the private room he had reserved. He did not mention his misadventures earlier that day.

As soon as the servers started clearing their plates, Cullen clicked his glass with a spoon and stood. "It's so good to have you here with me in Rome for this highly significant event in the life of the Archdiocese of Baltimore. Our local church is being honored, just as the pope is honoring me. I know it's been a long day, but I've asked my friend and church historian, Ian Landers, to give you an idea of what to expect at the consistory tomorrow and at the Mass on Sunday. And, if I know Ian, he will not be able to repress a few amusing historical facts."

Ian Landers stood, placed his napkin on his chair, and moved to a place where he could be better heard.

"The first thing you'll notice tomorrow is the absence of a eucharistic liturgy. A consistory is more like a liturgy of the word.

Following the procession—you might think it will never end—you'll see the pope kneel silently in prayer over the tomb of Saint Peter. Then one of the new cardinals will make an expression of homage and gratitude to the pope. An appropriate scripture reading will be followed by a papal address. He'll most likely speak in Italian, I fear, but the text of his remarks will be available in translation. The pope then will formally announce the names of the new cardinals. They'll stand, and in unison make a profession of faith and a vow of obedience to the pope. Then, one by one, the new cardinals will approach the pope to have him place upon their head their new red cardinal's biretta."

Landers took a sip of water and said, "Just a few historical points—as predicted—that you might find interesting. It's thought that the youngest cardinal ever appointed was just eight years old, the son of King Felipe V of Spain. This was in 1735. But earlier, Giovanni di Lorenzo de' Medici, who became Pope Leo X, was tonsured, that is, admitted into the clerical state, at age seven and named a cardinal at age thirteen. The pontiff who created the most cardinals was Pope John Paul II, who appointed a record 231 to the college." The crowd's interest seemed to be flagging; perhaps they were more tired than anything. *Best get on with it,* the professor thought.

"Right then. Let's move along quickly to the Mass the new cardinals will concelebrate with the pope on Sunday. During the Mass, they will receive from the pope their cardinals' rings and a document naming their titular church. Historically, cardinals were the pastors of local churches of Rome. Keeping with this tradition, each cardinal is assigned a different church in Rome, albeit with no real pastoral or administrative duties. The final aspect of this Mass worth mentioning is the kiss of peace, the *Pax Tecum.* Each of the new cardinals will exchange the kiss of peace with every cardinal present. Many find this very moving. Multitudes more find it interminable." Ian smiled. "Like my remarks, now, perhaps. So this seems a good place for a full stop."

Nora smiled at Ian when he took his seat. "Nice job, professor." After Bryn Martin offered a final prayer, she whispered to Ian, "Walk me back to my room?"

They walked in an awkward silence for a few minutes. "I think I know what's going on in that mind of yours, Nora. You're worried about Bryn and Cullen. But they're going to be fine. I have a good feeling about Tosco. And we'll likely soon learn the story behind that bloody text message."

"I pray you're right."

16

Dressed in a black clerical suit with an open-neck button-down shirt, Bryn Martin stood as instructed at the top of the alleyway next to the Café Sant'Eustachio. The Pantheon across the way was not yet closed for the evening. Martin scanned the Piazza della Rotonda.

Tosco had been right, the area around the Pantheon had a fair amount of foot traffic—mostly couples strolling arm in arm—and the piazza was well lit. If Tosco was nearby, Martin couldn't spot him, or anyone else who looked like an undercover cop. He took a step away from the entrance to the alleyway and consulted his watch. It was 9:10. A moment later he sensed someone approaching from behind.

"Bishop Martin?" a voice said in lightly accented English. Martin turned to see a man in his late fifties. "I'm glad you came." He wore a dark gray, pinstripe suit, white shirt, and conservative tie. He looked more like a banker or a successful businessman than a mob don.

"It will be chilly soon, I suggest we go inside. And we will have more privacy there."

They weaved through the café's half dozen small outdoor tables into a sleek coffee bar featuring the famous Eustachio label coffee. A young woman led the two men to an isolated table tucked into an alcove at the back of the café. Martin wondered if the table had been held open for them. Before sitting down, he glanced through the front window at the patrons seated at the outside tables. Young professionals, he thought, with a smattering of more-casually dressed men and women of college age. Tosco certainly wasn't among them. He wondered if he should have insisted on a sidewalk table.

Before either could say a word, a server approached.

"I recommend Eustachio's espresso," Scarano said. "There's really none better."

Martin nodded. "An espresso for me. With cream, please."

"*Espresso con panna, due, per favore,*" his companion told the waiter.

When the server was gone, the two men sat a moment in silent appraisal.

"I am so glad you agreed to meet me, Bishop Martin. Allow me to introduce myself. My name is Leonine Scarano. I expect you have been told I am the don of some violent criminal family here in Rome."

Martin, feeling his heart pulse, thought briefly of Sister Amelia DiRosa's revelations about the Scarano family business.

"Forgive me if I sound a bit defensive, but my family's activities are largely legitimate." Scarano's dark eyes softened. He seemed to be trying to say, Don't worry. You're safe with me. "We are in the restaurant business, in the food distribution business, especially wholesale fish, and we own a few vineyards." Scarano paused. "But we do have a few financial interests that I'll leave to your imagination." A hint of a smile crossed his face.

"Mr. Scarano," Martin said, "I know very well who you are. But why did you ask to meet?"

"Please, Bishop, call me Leo. I wanted to talk because you have come to know something about an organization secretly led by a man soon to be made a cardinal, Archbishop Pietro Montaldo."

He spoke the name with undisguised scorn.

Just as we suspected, Martin thought. *It had to be Montaldo.*

"Some of what I'm about to tell you, you will already have

surmised. In fact, that's exactly why you and Archbishop Cullen are in danger. You know too much. But hear me out. I want to make sure you see how adeptly the devil works in this evil man."

The server approached and placed a foam-topped espresso in front of each of them.

"Pietro Montaldo," Scarano said with apparent disdain, "is the most corrupt of a number of Vatican insiders who make the Mafia look like boy scouts. But he's put on the armor of a crusading knight on a mission to save the Holy Roman Catholic Church from anything modern, from anything that smacks of liberalism or secularism. But it's all a sham, Bishop. We know that Montaldo is only romanticizing the medieval church for his own financially corrupt purposes. He has idealized the *ancien régime*. He's a monarchist and probably sympathetic to fascism. But at heart he's a common crook. He wants the Catholic Church to become a religious empire whose power reaches everywhere, whose power controls everyone, not so he can help others, but so he can help himself."

Scarano took a sip of his espresso. The expression that crossed his face said, *I'm just getting started.*

Martin thought of Nora and Ian. Both, he knew, would affirm Scarano's assessment of Montaldo.

"Montaldo, Bishop Martin, is a man to be reckoned with. He has secret cells here in Italy and the States…in Spain, Poland, Hungary, and even Colombia. Until recently, only the leaders of these cells knew who their grand master was. Now, in many circles here in Rome, and even inside the Vatican, it is no secret that Montaldo is the supreme master behind them all."

Bryn Martin stirred uncomfortably in his chair, shrugging off the growing tension in his neck and shoulders. "Go on," he said, straining to keep his voice calm and his eyes focused intently on Scarano.

"I understand that you, Bishop Martin, have stumbled

onto two of these secret cells—one in Baltimore and another in Cleveland."

"How did you ever come to know about the cells in the States?"

Scarano smiled. "It's my business to know about corruption inside the walls of the Vatican. Their shady banking and financial dealings, their real estate maneuverings, the infiltration by the Masons, the 'Gentlemen of His Holiness' who exploit their access to the highest levels of Vatican power, the surprising number of Vatican priests and prelates who visit the city's prostitutes..." Scarano paused, "But I'm not answering your question, am I?"

"No, you aren't."

"The cell in Baltimore was under the local control of a former colleague of yours—Monsignor Aidan Kempe. He was, if my information is correct, the chancellor of the archdiocese and then financial secretary until he was demoted by Archbishop Cullen." Martin nodded. "Aidan Kempe panicked when he felt the Brotherhood of the Sacred Purple was about to be exposed because of the sexual exploitation of adolescent boys by the retired Archbishop of Baltimore, Wilfred Gunnison."

He even knows about Gunnison! Martin sat mesmerized.

"He flew to Rome then to consult with Montaldo. They met at the Borghese Gardens, not so far from here. Now Montaldo, like a number of other upper-level Vatican officials, has a driver, a very interesting driver. His name is Giorgio Grotti. This Grotti has an unusual résumé, Bishop. He's a former seminarian who got himself expelled for putting another seminarian in the hospital. A boy who made unwanted sexual advances. And he's a former carabiniere who was part of their elite GIS, their Special Intervention Group. We can be sure that he knows how to kill... efficiently and quietly. Montaldo's driver was sent off to Baltimore, in great haste, to remedy Kempe's difficulties there. You see, Giorgio Grotti is nothing less than Archbishop Montaldo's paid assassin."

"Tell me if I'm correct," Martin said. "Grotti is about six foot one, lean and athletic."

Scarano smiled. "You know him, then?"

"I have felt sure for a long time that Wilfred Gunnison, was murdered. And I'm pretty sure now, given what you've just told me, that Grotti was the killer."

"But your chancery issued a statement indicating the archbishop had taken his own life," Scarano said with a smirk.

"Yes…yes we did," Martin admitted. "You have quite an impressive intelligence network, Mr. Scarano."

Scarano squeezed a bit of lemon rind over his espresso. Pleased with Martin's compliment, Scarano decided to add some spice to his account.

"During the five years Kempe spent as a young priest studying canon law here in Rome, he regularly engaged with male prostitutes. When he came running to see Montaldo about the difficulties in Baltimore, he hooked up with a male escort, a *squillo*, as we call them. The escort happened to be on our payroll. We had no trouble putting the pieces together."

"You know Aidan Kempe is not here as a guest of Charles Cullen. He's here to celebrate the honor to be given Pietro Montaldo," Martin offered weakly.

Scarano considered just how frank to be. He knew more about Montaldo and Kempe, but he thought better of playing all his cards at once. "But now let's turn to your current diocese, Bishop. You no doubt wonder how we heard of the Cleveland cell, the Sentinels of the Supreme Center? As you know, it was a small cell, only a few bona fide members and a retired policeman recruited to do the heavy lifting."

"Small but deadly." Martin closed his eyes and thought of the murdered women priests, Laura Spivak and Frances Hellerman, and their dead assassin, Fergus Mann. *Clubbed to death in my stead by one Giorgio Grotti.*

Martin came back to the moment. "The core members of the Sentinels were Father Trace Dunmore, who I inherited as my chancellor when I was named Bishop of Cleveland," he said, with a note of sadness in his voice, "and a Renaissance art historian by the name of Simon Ashley."

Scarano looked at his manicured nails. "Montaldo loves art," he said. "Especially religious art, the classical stuff, not the modern junk. He fancies himself a collector of exquisite taste. He became obsessed with an illuminated missal created by two Perugian artists, the Caporali brothers, in the fifteenth century. Montaldo lusted after this piece as he did no other. One of Simon Ashley's tasks while he was in Cleveland was to persuade the Museum of Art to loan the *Caporali Missal* to the Archdiocese of Perugia. It's a good thing they did not. Believe me, Pietro would have appropriated it if the museum had ever lent it."

Martin sipped his lukewarm espresso. Scarano caught the eye of their waiter and signaled for two more.

"Montaldo had a second pressing interest in Cleveland," Scarano said. "The dozen or so women who claim to be validly ordained priests. Women priests are absolutely anathema to Montaldo and his inner circle. You know better than I, Bishop, the reign of terror he created. So, I heard about the events in Cleveland from both sides of the Atlantic. From my informants here and from my cousins in Cleveland."

Martin's head was spinning. He was awed at the depth of Scarano's knowledge of Montaldo's dark world. One unanswered question loomed large—why had Leonine Scarano decided to warn him? He opted to let Scarano take his time with that one.

"It will interest you to know, Bishop, that Montaldo's inner circle includes two very wealthy retired Cardinals, Alessandro Oradini and Andrea Vannucci, both living in princely splendor close to the walls of the Vatican. When his cash flow gets low, Pietro turns to them, and always gets what he needs."

So Montaldo manipulates great wealth, but has regular cash flow problems. Martin thought of Aidan Kempe's thefts from the Archdiocese of Baltimore when he was financial secretary to Charles Cullen.

Scarano seemed to savor waiting one delicious moment more before his last reveal. "Because he is blackmailing them both."

Martin tilted his head at the pronouncement. *Mother of mercy!*

"Here's the story as I understand it," Scarano continued. "Montaldo maintains an elaborate intelligence network within and outside the walls of the Vatican. He discovered that Oradini's and Vannucci's fathers had made a killing at the end of World War II and in the years immediately following. They were important bankers and used their positions to transfer to certain South American accounts the plundered wealth of fugitive Nazi officials. They arranged for forged passports and for passage out of Italy. The two *pappas* became very rich, and their wealth passed to their sons upon their deaths. And those sons' swift ascent up the clerical ladder was not at all inhibited by their great wealth."

Scarano went silent as their server walked towards their table with two fresh espressos.

"I heard back in my seminary days," Martin said, "of Catholic prelates and Catholic bankers and businessmen helping Nazi war criminals escape. A sad chapter in the church's history."

"Now Bishop...and this is only rumor...but the word in certain circles here is that Oradini's father and Vannucci's father," Leo looked over his shoulder, "may have spied for the Germans during the war. Maybe not true," Scarano's eyes sparkled, "but it adds spice to the story. Don't you think? What we do know is that Montaldo has only to ask, and Oradini and Vannucci deliver. The Vatican is rife with this kind of blackmail. Don't even get me started on the secret sexual dossiers Montaldo keeps. Such secrets are the real coin of the realm there. They open doors. They lead to luxury. They get one promoted."

"The Mafia and the church have something else in common," Martin said quietly. "*Omerta*. The silence that holds all secrets. This unholy silence, it's like a profane tabernacle that can never be opened. If it ever were, the whole institution might crumble."

"Precisely!" Scarano said with a knowing smile. "Precisely."

The waiter seated a young couple a few tables away. Scarano took his fresh espresso and downed it with a few gulps. "Shall we walk a bit, Bishop? The Piazza Navona is nearby. It's always lively at this time of the evening."

Martin sensed that Scarano liked him. And despite his reservations, he found himself falling under the considerable charm of this well-tailored don of a Mafia family, a man who knew a great deal more about the inner politics of the Vatican than Martin had ever imagined he might.

"Something else you should know about Pietro Montaldo," Scarano said as they strolled along the Corso del Rinascimento. "He controls a special purse, a very big purse, millions. He calls it the 'Papal Purse for the Poor.' It's off the books, so there's never any financial disclosure, but it's funded by very wealthy rightwing Catholics who want to return the church to the one, holy, *static*, religious empire of the Middle Ages. As far as we can discern, only about a third of the purse goes to charitable causes. A third goes to financing his secret networks. And a third, of course, goes to Montaldo himself. And generous cash gifts to high-ranking members of the curia are typically considered to be 'charitable causes' by many of these prelates."

Martin shook his head. "This makes Pietro Montaldo, soon

Cardinal Montaldo, a very powerful and very dangerous man."

Scarano took Martin's elbow. "That's one of the reasons I sent you a warning. It's why I wanted this meeting. You, and especially Cardinal Cullen, are among the few outsiders who are aware of just how toxic Montaldo is. And you're both in positions to resist his building of the kind of church that embraces his crazy theology."

They were at the Piazza Navona now and fell into a casual stroll around the striking fountains. The sounds of splashing water and lighthearted conversation lifted Martin's mood. He felt, to his surprise, safe. He looked to his right, and then to his left. No sign of Lorenzo Tosco or anyone who might be working for him.

"You're looking for Lorenzo Tosco, aren't you, my friend?

"As a matter of fact, I am."

"He's been with us all the time. From the moment we met outside the café. And so have a few of my own men. You, Bishop Martin, have never been quite so safe as you are now in the city of Rome."

Martin nodded. *Strange,* he thought. *I'm in the company of one of Rome's most notorious Mafia dons, yet I feel safe.*

"Tosco and I go back a ways," Scarano said. "We respect each other, maybe even like each other. You can trust him, Bishop. He hasn't been corrupted. Not even by me," he laughed.

"There's more I could tell you, Bishop, but I doubt we will have an opportunity to speak again."

"Explain then, why you sent me a warning."

"My answer is...complicated. And may leave you confused."

Martin scanned again the people seated at the outdoor tables or strolling around the Piazza. No sign of Lorenzo Tosco or his officers. Nor could he spot any of Scarano's people. But he didn't doubt for a moment that all of them had him in sight.

"So confuse me, Leo."

"In stark terms, our mutual enemy, Archbishop Montaldo, has ordered your assassination, and Cullen's. He sees both of you as threats to his dream of a spiritual empire in the name of Jesus Christ. And his 'driver,' Giorgio Grotti, is the man preparing to execute this order."

Martin slowed his pace. "This is not the first time Mondaldo has tried to kill me," he said. "The last attempt was thwarted by a decoy."

"So thanks be to God, Bishop, that you got another break. Grotti's asking us for help is quite unusual. In the past he's always acted alone."

Martin's sense of security began to slip away. He glanced nervously at the Fountain of Neptune, the rush of cascading rivulets of water there matching the sudden spurt of adrenalin in his chest.

"Maybe because he needs to accomplish two assassinations in just four days. It makes sense, I guess," Scarano said thoughtfully. "So he meets with someone in his line of work. And this someone, his misfortune, happens to work for me. I'll call him Aldo. My Aldo came to me and said he was asked to assist with your murder and the archbishop's." Scarano stopped and turned toward Martin. "I gave my blessing." Bishop Bryn Martin, frozen on the plaza, said nothing. "After giving my go-ahead, however, I decided it was a mistake. You and the archbishop have never hurt me. You aren't a threat to my businesses. I said to myself, 'Leo, what have you done?' So I told Aldo to pull out of his arrangement with Grotti. I wanted nothing to do with it. I was very clear. The family would have no part of this matter. Aldo was not a happy soldier. But he is loyal, and, most importantly, obedient. You have nothing to fear from the Scarano family, Bishop. Nothing."

"So you sent me a warning."

"Yes, I sent you a warning."

Good old-fashioned Catholic guilt, Martin thought. *It even exists in the heart of the Italian Mafia.*

Scarano looked relieved, like a man who has made a devout confession. "You must know, Bishop, that while you have nothing at all to fear from the Scarano family, I'm afraid you do have much to fear from Giorgio Grotti. The man is a born killer."

17

Later that evening, Nora Martin sat next to her brother on the couch in Charles Cullen's suite. Ian sat on the edge of the king-size bed, leaving one of the two upholstered chairs for Cullen. The other was reserved for Inspector General Lorenzo Tosco, who was expected momentarily. They were all sipping scotch from crystal tumblers, but there was an urn of hot coffee on the credenza. Their very long Friday was far from over.

Ian answered a light knock on Cullen's door. It was Tosco.

"I didn't see you tonight, Inspector, but I was sure you were close by," Martin said, looking drained.

Tosco smiled, "Yes, we had you covered all the way. And so did Scarano's men. You appeared to be deep in conversation, and I'm anxious to hear about it." Lorenzo spotted the scotch and the coffee. "It's been a long day. May I help myself to some coffee?"

"Yes, of course," Cullen said graciously.

Tosco poured his coffee, settled into his chair, and pressed the "Record" button on a small digital voice recorder. He turned toward Martin and said, "So...?"

"You know this, Inspector, but the others don't. The man I met tonight is Leonine Scarano, the don of the Scarano family. There is reason to be concerned. Pietro Montaldo has ordered that Charles and I be assassinated within the next three days. Montaldo thinks we know too much about his secret societies. So we do need to be careful. Scarano says our assailant will be Montaldo's personal driver, a former carabiniere by the name of

Giorgio Grotti."

"I know that name. I seem to remember some history of violent behavior. The Carabinieri and the Polizia di Stato will both have files on him," Tosco said. He took out a smart phone and tapped something into it.

Martin got up, walked to the desk in the suite and picked up a 9 x 12 envelope. "This was waiting for me when I got back to the hotel. It's a fax from two friends of mine in Baltimore, George Havel and Duane Moore." Martin looked to Tosco. "Havel is a retired CIA agent. Moore is a former special agent of the FBI. I asked them to do some digging before I left Cleveland to see what they could find out about a man we know only as Monsignor Giancarlo Foscari, a supposed emissary from the Vatican. This Foscari was in Baltimore the night Archbishop Gunnison was murdered. A day later he threatened a colleague, Margaret Comiskey, who is here in the hotel. It was Margaret who first stumbled onto the secret society in Baltimore." Martin stopped short. "I'm afraid I may be getting ahead of myself."

"You're doing just fine, Bishop," Tosco responded, lifting his glance from his smart phone.

"Havel and Moore have confirmed that this Foscari is, in fact, Giorgio Grotti. Manifests show that right after Gunnison's death, Grotti flew from Baltimore to Bogota, Colombia, and hid out in a convent there. After three months he went back to Rome and assumed his duties as Montaldo's *driver*. That is, Montaldo's *assassin*." Tosco stirred in his chair. "How did Leonine Scarano discover Montaldo's intentions?"

"Grotti felt he needed some help in pulling off his assignment to kill Charles and me in the few days we'll be here in Rome, and he turned to a member of the don's family. Scarano at first approved of helping Grotti, but later changed his mind. Scarano really has no use for Montaldo, and decided he doesn't want the family involved with him. So he backed out."

"But why send you a warning?" Nora persisted.

"Catholic guilt," Bryn said, shrugging.

"There are many men in Rome who would be happy to accept Grotti's business," Tosco added. "He knew you would still be in danger."

"It is plausible that the don wants Montaldo to fail," Ian said. "That he wants his schemes to go all to pot."

"That makes perfect sense," said Tosco.

The room went silent for a moment.

"Inspector," the archbishop said, "I know you're going to provide as much security as you can. And we appreciate that. But can't your Gendarmes or the Carabinieri find some reason to arrest and hold Grotti until we leave?"

"There may be a way. We'd all feel better if Grotti was in custody while you are in Rome. But we can't arrest a man for what he is about to do. But inventing a pretext to hold him would be the easy part. We have to find him first. Montaldo's official party is at the Cavalieri, the Waldorf Astoria hotel. I've seen his guest list. I don't remember seeing Grotti's name on it. He could be anywhere in the city."

Martin stood and paced around the suite. "Grotti could be across the street right now, waiting for you to leave. There must be some way we can make him step out of the shadows and come to us."

"We have one distinct leg up," Ian offered. "Grotti has no idea we have identified him."

"What if Charles and I invite him to make his move? Create a situation in which we appear vulnerable?"

Lorenzo Tosco remained seated but spoke deliberately and with authority. "Bishop, I admire your courage. But that kind of operation is extremely dangerous. There's always a chance your security personnel wouldn't get to you in time. We have no idea what Grotti's next move will be. What if he decides to strike from a distance? His Carabinieri file notes he's an expert marksman," he said, holding aloft his smart phone. Consulting it again, swiping down the screen, he said, "He was first in his class. Trained as a special ops officer." He closed the screen on his phone. "Grotti knows a dozen ways to kill you. Moreover, my force is pretty much wrapped up in providing security for the consistory. I don't have the personnel to cover the kind of sting you're suggesting. And I'm not sure what kind of assistance I could get from the Carabinieri."

Martin said simply, "I see."

"I'll have the Vatican Gendarmerie, the Carabinieri, and Polizia di Stato alerted to seek and detain Grotti as a material witness in an ongoing criminal conspiracy. If we can get him into custody, I'll find some excuse to hold him until you're on your way back to the States. But there is a limit to what we can do."

Martin rubbed his eyes and sighed, "Your right, Inspector. Maybe, under our current circumstances, the best offense is a good defense."

"We will do our best, Bishop. You two need to keep yourselves as safe as possible. Double-lock your doors, don't open them to anyone. No room service. Decline housekeeping requests. Keep your blinds drawn. Stay away from the windows. You have my cell number and I have yours. Call me immediately if you sense something isn't quite right. I'll call you around ten in the morning." Tosco managed a smile. "Sleep well," he said weakly.

18

Vittoria Massi pulled the bedsheet up to her chin, more as if to ward off the night's chill than to cover her nakedness. Her tumble with Giorgio Grotti had been disappointing. She had been having sex with him rather than Grotti having sex with her. But she was used to being the dominant.

"You're still angry, aren't you?"

Grotti was pulling on his pants. "Of course, I'm still angry. Angelo, you, me…we had a deal. But your don does a flip flop. And this," Grotti pointed his chin at the disheveled bed, "this was a mistake. I don't have time for this."

Massi wondered if she should feel insulted.

"Yes, it's really too bad," she said. "The archbishop's death—I should say, the cardinal's death—would have looked like a heart attack. The potassium chloride would have done the trick without leaving a wisp of evidence. That would have left you with only the bishop to take care of."

Grotti sat on the edge of the bed, slipping on his Dolce & Gabbana loafers. "I'll eliminate both of them. You'll see."

"So you have a Plan B?"

"I always have a Plan B," he lied. But he had to get out of Massi's bedroom and start working on a solo strategy. "I will need to stay in your apartment the next two nights. All right?"

"The don wouldn't like it if he found out. He doesn't want me or Angelo to have anything to do with you."

"I'm certainly not going to tell him," Grotti said as he slammed the door to her bedroom behind him.

Giorgio Grotti, missing the irony of it, strode with an erect military gate down the Via dell'Umiltà, the narrow, cobbled Street of Humility, his strutting an unconscious attempt to repress the emptiness and pain he felt inside. His pace slowed as he began to wrestle with his darkest angels. He passed the Trevi Fountain, almost free of tourists on this chilly night. From time to time he stopped to get his bearings, like a tourist meandering in a strange city. A few blocks later, near the Piazza dell'Oratorio, he sat down at a sidewalk table in front of a closed trattoria, his stomach, like his soul, empty and complaining. Most everything was closed down and Grotti felt a churchlike silence closing around him. From somewhere…from nowhere…he felt an uncommon urge rising in his chest. An urge to pray. He laughed at himself, the failed seminarian. *What a crazy idea.*

It had rained while he had been in bed with Massi, and the street—sleek and shimmering in its watered freshness—smelled clean and pure. From somewhere out of the darkness came the aroma of baking bread. Grotti breathed in the comforting smells. Resting his elbows on the metal table, he buried his face in his hands. He couldn't remember ever feeling quite so lost, quite so impotent. The embarrassment of his poor performance with Massi still stung. That would pass. He was feeling stupid for not recognizing that Montaldo was gay, and worse, that he preyed on young men. Homosexuals disgusted him. But right now, in the pre-morning darkness, uppermost in his heart was a sense of betrayal and anger with Angelo Correa over the broken deal. The jumble of emotions stirred the juices of Grotti's growling stomach. Maybe his rage was more directed at himself than at Correa or Montaldo.

In spite of the urgent need to develop a new plan, he sat quietly, like a penitent awaiting the cleansing of confession. Montaldo had urged him, over the years, to think of himself as a warrior-knight, fighting to protect his religion. And the only religion for Grotti was the Holy Roman Catholic Church. And he had proven a good and faithful soldier. But he saw now, for the first time really, that good soldiers only kill other good soldiers. And defenders of one faith only kill defenders of another. Maybe Montaldo's heretics were just good people searching for God as best they could. What, in God's holy name, had he been doing these past few years? *Am I a stalwart soldier in the army of the Lord? Or just another hired assassin?* Grotti arrived at an unsettling truth. He had lost his faith in the name of protecting his religion.

But now, as a faithless and fallen soldier-knight, he had to think and to think hard. He got up slowly and started walking, feeling as if he were plodding straight into a moment of truth. And in that moment, a plan began to take shape, arriving like unmerited grace from his darker angels. Like an artist waiting for the voice of his muse, Grotti let his thoughts softly unfurl. A plan came into focus. He had learned long ago that the best plans are not forced. You have to let them come to you. He remembered reading once how that was Napoleon's way of preparing for a battle. Think hard, calculate well, plan carefully—and then wait and let both strategy and tactics come to you. Yes, that was Napoleon's genius. A dialectic of intelligence and intuition, of shrewdness and inspiration. And a plan was developing clearly now in his soldier's eye. No, not a Plan B. A fresh, completely new Plan A. With each step, Grotti knew with mounting clarity what he must do. And to his relief, the familiar erotic rush, the focused excitement of a skilled assassin preparing to strike, surged in his veins.

19

Bishop Bryn Martin took the first open table he saw in the Hotel Raphael's breakfast room. He scanned the entrance for Charles, who had phoned to say he would be heading down shortly. Martin, dying for a cup of coffee after a few hours of sleep, looked up to see a server moving toward his table with a carafe.

"Are you by yourself?" the waitress asked in lightly accented English.

"I'm waiting for one other guest."

Unbidden, she poured a cup of black Americano and left the carafe on the table. After a few restorative sips of coffee, Martin looked around the restaurant and the lobby it opened onto. He settled his attention on the people in the lobby, trying to spot an out-of-uniform carabiniere or one of Tosco's gendarmes. Charles Cullen walked into the room and Martin caught his eye.

"Good morning, Bryn," Cullen said as he sat down. "How did you sleep?"

"Fitfully. How about you?"

"Pretty much the same," Cullen answered, noticing that Martin's attention was on the lobby. "I bet our protection detail is the young woman in the workout suit, looking like she's waiting for a taxi. The roller case next to her is a nice touch," he said confidently.

Martin said, with a thin smile, "You might be right."

Cullen poured himself a cup of coffee. "Is there a menu?"

"It seems to be buffet only. I'm going to see what they're offering," Martin said as he got up to move to the buffet. He didn't quite make it. Many of the patrons in the restaurant were Cullen's friends and family or other members of his official party. Martin found Margaret Comiskey at a table close to the buffet, sitting with Ian and his mother, Ella Landers.

"Good morning," Martin said with genuine warmth. "How are you two?"

"Adjusting to jetlag, but overall feeling okay," Ella said. "And you?"

Before the bishop could respond, Ella said, "Please sit down, Bryn, just for a minute. Nora is on her way down to join us." Martin took the empty fourth chair at their table.

"I'm okay, too," he said. "Out of sorts from the flight, but happy for Charles. I'm sorry I didn't get a chance to visit with you two ladies at the airport or during the flight. There have been some...distractions," Martin said with a knowing look to Ian. Cullen and Martin had decided not to tell Ella or Margaret of the warning, reasoning they were in no danger and deserved to have as pleasant an experience as their short visit to Rome allowed. Martin leaned in, "You probably saw that Aidan Kempe was on our flight."

"We sure did," Margaret said with a distinct note of anxiety in her voice. "We didn't meet on the plane, but we saw each other going through customs. He looked right through me, like I was invisible."

Ella said nothing, but put her hand over Margaret's.

Sensing her fear of a confrontation, Martin said, "There's no way to escape the awkwardness of this situation, Margaret. But in my eyes, and in the eyes of Charles Cullen, you're a hero. Remember that. You've got more integrity in your little finger than Kempe has in his whole body. But here's the sad truth. Kempe has no compunction whatsoever about what he's done. He thinks of himself as a knight in shining armor. We have to recognize that, as sick as it is. So walk tall, Margaret. You shouldn't have too many encounters with him this weekend. Maybe none at all. He is here to bask in the light of his hero, Pietro Montaldo." Martin turned to Ella. "I know you'll stay close to Margaret until we're away from him."

"Of course," Ella said, patting Margaret's hand.

"If it weren't for you two, Charles and I would never have caught on to the Brotherhood of the Sacred Purple, never known how truly dangerous Montaldo is."

Margaret said with a polite smile, "Thank you, Bryn. That really helps. But my experiences with Aidan Kempe, and what I've since learned about Montaldo, make me wonder about our church, the institutional church, and our bishops. Present company excluded, of course. Thank God for men like you and Charles."

"Bryn," said Ella, "Margaret and I know the church and its politics better than most laypeople. Margaret, more than I, of course. But I don't understand how a man like Montaldo could rise through the ranks to be named a cardinal."

"I have some thoughts on that, Ella. But I'm going to save them for the flight home. Right now ought to be a time for celebration. Let's try to enjoy being in Rome as much as we can for the few days we are here. You're free until the coaches leave for the basilica at two."

On the way back with a wedge of frittata and a small slice of tea cake, Martin found Cullen with Margaret, Ella, and Ian, standing next to their table, chatting amiably. He hardly looked rested, but Martin knew him to be a man who would rise to overcome the scary drama engulfing them.

20

Later that morning, Inspector General Tosco, Bishop Martin, and Archbishop Cullen sat in a quiet corner of the Hotel Raphael's lobby, their chairs pulled into a tight triangle.

"We've checked the hotels and hostels of the city," said Tosco. "No sign of Grotti. Or anyone named Foscari. We sent his Carabinieri photo to their registration desks. He's probably too smart to leave a hotel record of his presence in Rome. He'd sleep in his car first."

"He must be close," Cullen said, furrowing his brow. "Maybe laying low in sight of our hotel."

"That's the challenge." Tosco said. "He could be anywhere."

"Can't you arrest Montaldo?" Martin asked. "We know that he ordered Grotti to kill us. If you arrested him, he might call his man off."

"We just don't have enough hard evidence to do that. We've only *heard* about a plan to murder you and the archbishop. You might be surprised, but we get tips like this—usually without substance—on a fairly regular basis."

This is far from some anonymous tip, Martin thought, but bit his tongue. It would be just too embarrassing to the Holy See for the Vatican police to arrest a cardinal-elect just hours before he was to be formally admitted to the College of Cardinals. He and Cullen exchanged a troubled glance.

Tosco broke the brief silence. "We have cameras throughout the Vatican. In Saint Peter's, the piazza, the museums, the Vatican Palace. We'll be watching monitors covering every aspect of the consistory. Our uniformed and plainclothes gendarmes and the Swiss Guard have been alerted that an attempt may be made on your lives. All of our security personnel, including the Guard, will be able to communicate instantly with one another in the event of trouble. And I'll be in constant contact with the Carabinieri officer leading security details in the piazza and surrounding areas. They're armed with Glock 17s and some, at key stations, with the more powerful Beretta M12. Don't worry. We're ready."

"I know you are," Cullen said, with evident gratitude in his voice.

"Archbishop," Tosco said, "I'm sorry this…this tension… hangs over a day that should be a most happy one for you. If it is any comfort to know, Officer Corsi will drive you two from your hotel to Saint Anne's Gate of the Vatican. He'll be in the lobby at 1:45."

"Thank you, Inspector," Cullen said sincerely, shaking the inspector's hand and covering their joined hands with his left. Then, with his penchant for dark humor, Cullen thought to himself, *Lord, just get me to the church on time!*

21

Aidan Kempe, Tom Fenton, and Herm Volker settled into their outdoor chairs at Bernini Ristorante, one of the numerous restaurants surrounding the Piazza Navona.

"When I was doctoral student here," Kempe said, enjoying the relief from the afternoon sun offered by the umbrella over their table, "I never tired of the energy and architecture of this piazza."

He ordered for the table: a bottle of Barolo, an antipasto plate, pasta Bolognese, and roast chicken. "Make this your main meal, gentlemen. You won't be fed again until after the reception, around eight or so."

For Kempe, this was a bittersweet visit to the Holy City. His reign as the leader of the Brotherhood of the Sacred Purple had ended abruptly after the death of Wilfred Gunnison. He missed the sense of purpose, not to mention the power, the secret fraternity had given him. Among the priests of Baltimore, he had once been a force to be reckoned with. He influenced the appointment of pastors, the assignment of associates, and decided who would be sent off to Rome for graduate degrees. And he was friendly, some said too friendly, with northern Maryland's high society. He had been the number-two man at the archdiocese. He awarded lucrative contracts to architects, contractors, engineers, and realtors. And with the cultivated social grace and reserve of a United States senator, he moved easily among the Catholic country-club set across ten counties, from the panhandle to the Chesapeake.

When the antipasto platter arrived, Kempe picked at it without pleasure. What did he miss most? The sense of purpose, or the power? To Kempe, the two were one and the same. He knew he used his power only to keep the church Catholic, to keep it orthodox. A noble purpose that too few priests understood. He and fellow priests of the Brotherhood had worked quietly and successfully to make sure conservative, safe men were appointed bishops. And they were succeeding until Wilfred Gunnison's venality brought it all down. Now he was a pastor of an obscure parish in the mountains of western Maryland. He brooded in silence through the meal.

"We have fallen so far," he said to Fenton and Volker as the waiter cleared their pasta bowls. "I pray Archbishop Montaldo's induction into the College of Cardinals will give our movement new life. That would be a sweetness beyond tasting."

Volker, for his part, was thrilled just to be in Rome, awestruck at the physical beauty of the city, awaiting eagerly the reward for his dogged loyalty, attending his first consistory in Saint Peter's Basilica. "But you accomplished so much when the order came to suppress the Brotherhood, Aidan. You kept us all out of trouble with Cullen and Martin."

Kempe permitted himself a small smile of pleasure. *Yes, I did swiftly and efficiently minimize our losses. Surely that counts for something.*

"Some of us still get together," Fenton added. "But just as priests having a good meal together. That special feeling of belonging to a fraternity of men bound together to protect the faith…that's gone."

"And we once had our own grand master, right in the heart of the Vatican," Volker said in almost a whisper. "That added to the mystique."

They fell silent as their entrees were set before them, and ate in silence while Kempe considered how much to share.

"I was forbidden to tell you at the time," Kempe said finally, reaching for his wine, "that our Roman patron and leader, M, was Archbishop Montaldo. He was adamant about that. Not even Wilfred Gunnison knew. But among us now, the secret is out. But that presents no real risk to Montaldo or to those of us doing the hard work of executing our mission. We have been smart enough to hide our membership records and obscure our actions. But that has kept the rest of us invisible as his star keeps rising."

"Will we get to meet him?" Fenton asked.

"Right after the consistory. The cardinal will host a *visite di cortesia*. Maybe later in the evening we will have some private time with him. Back at the hotel." Kempe glanced at each of them. "But don't count on it. We're far from being in his inner circle."

Herm Volker swallowed a bite of the chicken, sipped his wine, and asked, "What can you tell us about the brotherhood in Cleveland, the Sentinels of the Supreme Center?"

"Brotherhood is a stretch. Just two men, really. One a layman, who was Montaldo's contact, an art historian who taught at John Carroll. His name is Simon Ashley. The other is an Anglican convert, a Father Trace Dunmore, who was already chancellor of the Cleveland diocese when Bryn Martin arrived. You'll meet them this evening. Ashley and Dunmore recruited—seduced might be a better word—a retired Cleveland policeman to carry out a plan to terrorize women who had found a rogue bishop to ordain them priests. The idea was to stop this heretical practice once and for all. That's all I should say. The less you know about that mess the better."

Volker and Fenton exchanged a dark glance.

Kempe went on. "That group, the Sentinels of the Supreme Center, has also been dissolved. Unfortunately, Charles Cullen and Bryn Martin know far too much about both brotherhoods.

They and their ilk have little regard for Catholic truth and orthodoxy. They're both liberal, Vatican II types committed to making the church what they deem to be relevant. What they're really doing is making the church Protestant."

Fenton and Volker nodded their agreement.

"We need to get back to the hotel," Kempe said, getting up and tossing his napkin down on the table with a bit of force, "It's a damn disgrace that a man like Charles Cullen is being made a cardinal. What were they thinking?"

22

Is this Father Tom Hathaway?" Ian said into his cell phone.

"Yes. Who's calling please?"

"Tom, it's Ian Landers. I mentioned I'd be here in Rome for the consistory. Any chance we can meet for coffee?"

"Sure. What's a good time for you?"

"This is a trifle nervy of me, but how about right now? I have some time before I need to leave for the consistory and the matter I'd like to discuss has grown quite urgent."

"Why don't you come to the Angelicum for lunch? I'll reserve a quiet table in the refectory for the two of us. I suspect you'd like some privacy."

"Perfect! I can be there in half an hour."

The Pontifical University of Saint Thomas Aquinas, more commonly known as the Angelicum, was situated, fittingly enough, on the Largo Angelicum, in the heart of Rome. Tom Hathaway was waiting for Ian at the main entrance.

"Tom, it is so good of you to see me on such short notice."

"You caught me at a good time. We don't have classes on Saturdays, and hardly any on Fridays, so this works out quite well. And I always enjoy your insights about this struggling church of ours. We'll eat in the friars' dining room. Not exactly up to Oxford's standards, but it has its own ambience."

Twenty minutes later, over soup and a plate of carbonara, the two had mostly caught up on professional matters. Landers had described his work in the history department of Johns Hopkins and Hathaway his place on the Angelicum's theology faculty.

"Tell me, Ian, are you married?" Hathaway asked.

"No, I'm not, but there is someone I'm quite close to. A very significant other, as they say in the States. Her name is Nora Martin. She's a fascinating woman. Before joining the psychology department at Johns Hopkins, she was a Carmelite nun—a cloistered Carmelite nun. Her particular gift is wedding sound psychology with authentic spirituality, especially contemplative spirituality. Her brother, Bryn, is the Bishop of Cleveland. We are all here for the consistory. Charles Cullen of Baltimore is getting a red hat."

Pushing his plate aside and pausing as if for dramatic effect, Landers said, "One of the two courses I'm teaching this semester is on the secret societies of the Middle Ages. I have now become aware of *two* such secret, malignant, societies linked to Pietro Montaldo."

"If you could spend even a few weeks in Rome," Hathaway responded, "you would soon learn all about such cliques, mostly informal, mostly small and ineffectual. But the social lives of a lot of priests and bishops revolve around them."

"I have no doubt," Landers said. He consulted his watch. "The consistory starts at three, so I have to watch the time. But what you once shared with me about Montaldo squares with what I've learned about him on my own. But he's far worse than just another conservative longing for the old days. He's the leader of an underground movement to root out liberal—he would say heretical—priests and bishops by any means."

Hathaway added, "And push the careers of bishops who think as he does. And stymie the progress of those who do not."

"I wish it were just that, Tom. This man is ruthless. Lives may be in danger."

"Most priests and bishops in the Vatican are actually afraid of him," Hathaway said in a lowered voice. "I can't really say that about any of the other power prelates. But I can about Archbishop Pietro Montaldo. And in just a few hours, *Cardinal* Montaldo.

"About half of my students," Hathaway continued, "are seminarians." He lowered his voice still further. "I discreetly advise them to keep their distance from Montaldo. He has a reputation for hitting on them. I'm glad to have him out of Rome, but feel bad for the church in Perugia. Now that he has his little red hat, I guess he'll be spending a lot more time back here."

Landers glanced at his watch again. "Listen, I have to get going, but thanks for confirming what I've come to know about Montaldo. My own archbishop, Charles Cullen, is getting his red hat, too, as I mentioned. They're not exactly stamped from the same coin."

"You don't say," Hathaway said with unrestrained irony.

"And I come with a last-minute invitation to join Cardinal Cullen for a celebratory dinner tomorrow evening at La Compana. It's on—"

"I know the place well. Thanks. I'll be there. What time?"

"We'll be gathering on the early side for Rome, about 6:30. And dinner comes with a bonus. I'll introduce you to Ms. Nora Martin."

23

Pietro Gonzaga Montaldo stood in the center of his bedroom in one of the Presidential Suites of Rome's Cavalieri Hotel, the light from the early afternoon sun filling the room with a soft aura of celestial light. His cardinal's robes fit perfectly, as he had made sure they would, and for long minutes he stood gazing with unabashed vanity into a floor-length mirror. A bit too much lace in his surplice, his *cotta*, perhaps. But the lace contributed to the persona he wanted to project. He at last looked every bit the prince of the church he was about to become. Overall, he found himself quite satisfied with these outward manifestations of his inner sanctitude. *And there is no doubt I would look equally regal in white*, he thought. But that, by the grace of God, would come in due time. Now he must dwell fully in the moment. The church was honoring and, more importantly, sustaining his legacy. He thought of his mother, Maria Gonzaga. A gracious, kind woman descended from a distinguished bloodline that boasted bishops, cardinals, and even a saint among its number. "St. Aloysius Gonzaga, pray for me," he said half aloud. And the Montaldos, his father's ancestors, had been prosecutors of the Inquisition, protecting the church's holy mission with fierce fidelity through the horrors of the Reformation. After today, he would have a clear, divine mandate to protect and defend the church his family had served with fortitude—and whatever force was necessary—for six hundred years. *Ad Majorem Dei Gloriam!*

Two taps on his door brought Montaldo back to the moment. "Come in."

Father Trace Dunmore entered the suite, followed by Simon Ashley.

Montaldo moved away from the mirror but remained standing to avoid wrinkling his cardinal's robes.

"You look so regal, *Eminenza*," Dunmore said.

Ashley nodded his approval at the aptness of the comment, and in appreciation of the sycophantic grin that accompanied it.

"Father Dunmore, I've made a minor change for the consistory. I've asked Monsignor Kempe to serve as my secretary. I know you may have inferred the honor would be yours. I understand you might be disappointed."

Dunmore stiffened. As Montaldo's master of ceremonies in Perugia, it was not an "inference" that he would act as secretary at the consistory. It was his right. The priest said nothing aloud, but the blotches of color flooding his cheeks spoke volumes. Ashley instinctively stepped back a half step, as if to be safely out of the line of fire.

"You see, Father, Monsignor Kempe has been banished to the backwoods of the Baltimore diocese by his archbishop, an undeserving man unfortunately soon also to be made a cardinal archbishop. I need for Cardinal Cullen to see that a priest he has chosen to scorn is in favor with the Cardinal Archbishop of Perugia."

"Whatever you say, Eminence," Dunmore said in his clipped British accent, with the slightest bow of his head.

Ashley said nothing but arched one eyebrow as if finding the little drama immensely entertaining.

"I knew you would understand, Father," Montaldo said with affected gentility.

Setting his shoulders back and seeming to swallow Montaldo's disregard like the British aristocrat he was, Dunmore announced formally, "It's time for his Eminence to leave for the basilica."

24

Vested in his cardinal's robes, Charles Cullen sat uncomfortably in his Raphael Hotel suite. Bryn Martin waited with him. Both men, sipping bottled water, were feeling wary.

"Things will go smoothly, Charles. We have the Vatican Gendarmerie and the Carabinieri alerted and ready to address anything unusual."

"I almost wish Scarano had never sent you that text."

Martin managed a smile that said, *I'm not so sure.* "Grotti won't try anything during the consistory. That would spoil his boss's big moment."

"I've thought of that," Cullen said, with a sigh of relief. "I think the same about the Mass tomorrow. Montaldo won't want a Papal Mass marred either."

Martin raised an eyebrow, and left his next thought unspoken. *But Grotti is cunning, skilled, and smart. He could try to get at us at any time.*

"Still," Cullen said, "we better make sure Tosco and his team have our backs until the moment we pass through airport security on Tuesday. I don't think I'll relax until we're all in the air."

Martin nodded, "I'll make sure of that."

The room phone rang. When Martin answered, the desk clerk reported that a Carabinieri car was outside the hotel waiting to take them to Saint Peter's Basilica.

"Let's get this show on the road," Cullen said. They headed

to the elevators. When the elevator door opened onto the lobby, they were greeted by a smiling Paolo Corsi, Cullen's shadow, not in his police uniform, but dressed in a cassock and surplice.

"Cardinal Cullen," Corsi said proudly, "the Inspector persuaded the director of the Office for Pontifical Ceremonies to let me serve as your secretary. I will be within six feet of you the whole time you are out."

Corsi didn't add that he was secreting an 18-round Beretta 92 under the folds of his cassock.

Inspector General Lorenzo Tosco had been faced with a difficult choice. He could monitor the consistory from the better-equipped Gendarmerie Corps headquarters on Via del Pellegrino, a short drive from Saint Peter's, or from a suite of discreet offices that served as an onsite command station on a lower floor of the Apostolic Palace. In light of the threat to the two American bishops, given weight by the don of the Scarano family, he decided to remain inside the walls of the Vatican. More importantly, he wanted Bryn Martin at his side.

Bishop Bryn Martin, dressed in his *filettata*, a black cassock with the red buttons, piping, and sash, moved toward the section of the basilica reserved for bishops and archbishops. Before he could sit down, a Swiss Guard, dressed in his less formal dark blue uniform, approached him.

"Bishop Martin?"

"Yes, what is it?"

"Please come with me."

The guard led Martin to the elevator near the back of the basilica's right transept. Only when the doors closed and the elevator began its descent, did he speak again. "The Commander of the Gendarmerie, Inspector Tosco, has requested your presence, Bishop."

Martin was led through an unmarked door into a dimly lit room with a dozen video monitors watched by three uniformed policemen.

Tosco seemed to step out of the shadows. "I wanted to have another set of eyes here in the command station. I assumed you would be willing to watch the consistory from here, Bishop."

"Yes, of course, Inspector." Martin followed Tosco a few steps closer to the monitors. Most of the cameras covered the basilica, but some were focused on Saint Peter's Square, where a sizable crowd of nuns, priests, tourists, and locals waited for the consistory to begin.

Tosco and Martin stood shoulder to shoulder behind the seated officers. As Martin's eyes adjusted to the darkened room he scanned slowly from screen to screen.

Tosco, speaking softly, said, "The personnel here have an open line with the gendarmes both inside and outside Saint Peter's. And I have a channel open to the captain in charge of the Carabinieri unit assigned to the consistory, some uniformed and some in plain clothes. Their eyes will be mostly on the crowds in the square."

Martin knew that consistories were not open to the public, and that the jumbo screen in Saint Peter's Square would make the ceremony available to those without tickets.

"This all looks really high tech," he said to the inspector.

Tosco nodded at the compliment and glanced at the wall clock. 2:35. "The north—or right—transept," he pointed to one of the screens, "has been cordoned off as a vesting and gathering area for the participating cardinals and bishops."

Martin spotted Cullen quickly, the only American to be installed in the college, standing alone. Both Martin and Tosco smiled when they saw Cullen glancing furtively at the tiny camera halfway up one of the columns of the basilica, focused on the right transept. *Yes, we're watching, Charles. Everything's looking normal.*

Tosco studied his officers. Each was paying close attention to his assigned screens, looking for anything the least bit unusual. "We're as ready as we possibly can be," he said.

Cullen stood, alone with his worries, in the north transept. Montaldo, thankfully, had his back to him. He wondered what he would say to the man when they came face to face. Montaldo looked poised and self-assured, fully engrossed in his role as a new Prince of the Church. Many of the new cardinals seemed monk-like, humbled by the honor about to fall on them. But a few could barely hide their pleasure at achieving a status they had lusted after for decades. The master of ceremonies asked for their attention and described how they would process into the main nave in twos. He paired them up and assigned each couple their respective place in the procession.

Cullen suspected Montaldo was as dismayed as he was when the master of ceremonies announced the two of them would be processing into the consistory shoulder to shoulder. Neither spoke a word to the other, making only the briefest eye contact as they lined up for the processional. *This is it, Charlie,* Cullen said to himself, half doubting it could be true.

25

Nora Martin, Ian Landers, his mother, Ella, and her friend Margaret Comiskey had front-row seats in the left transept of the basilica. Florence and Marcus Merriman were in place just a few chairs behind them. In the basilica's spacious sanctuary they could see twelve brocaded armchairs set two feet apart in a half circle directly in front of the pope's chair, six on each side of the sanctuary. Directly behind these chairs, another half circle of twelve chairs were being filled by the secretaries appointed to assist the new cardinals. Most of the cardinals, bishops, and priests attending the consistory were already in place. The attending cardinals, a mass of scarlet in their ecclesial robes, were seated a few yards behind the secretaries.

Margaret Comiskey leaned into Ella Lander's shoulder and whispered, "If Archbishop Cullen sits on the right side, he'll be right in our line of sight during the ceremony."

The Cappella Musicale Pontificia, the pope's personal choir, raised their voices in an uplifting processional hymn as the cross-bearer led the twelve new cardinals, two abreast, slowly up the center aisle of the basilica. Margaret and Ella, moved by the transcendent purity and rich harmonies of boy's and men's voices lifted in praise, gasped aloud when they saw the second pair of cardinals, walking side by side, just inches apart, coupled by some devilish or divine design. In perfect synchrony, Cullen and Montaldo bowed before the huge main altar and turned to take their chairs, Montaldo going to the right and Cullen to the left.

"I'm afraid, Margaret," Ella whispered, "we'll have a good view of Montaldo, but only a profile of Charles."

"And a bird's eye view of Aidan Kempe," Comiskey said a bit louder than she had intended. "Ella, look, Kempe is right behind Montaldo. He's his secretary! That's a deliberate poke in the eye to Charles."

Nora Martin couldn't take her eyes off Montaldo. Like Cullen, Montaldo looked to be twenty pounds overweight. But Montaldo's shoulders were back, giving him an almost military bearing. So here, before her, stood the grand master of at least two secret societies, the Brotherhood of the Sacred Purple and the Sentinels of the Supreme Center. She would learn everything she could from his body language. She turned to Ian. "Have you spotted Bryn?"

"Not yet," he replied. "He must be out of our line of sight. It's one of the disadvantages of being seated here. We'll be lucky to catch a glimpse of the pope, what with the columns of this bloody Baldacchino in the way."

Lorenzo Tosco checked in with his squad leaders. "No signs of Grotti," he said to Martin. Nothing obviously out of place. I'm getting the same report from the Carabinieri." But both men continued to steadfastly scan the banks of video screens.

Giorgio Grotti, dressed in a priest's cassock, sporting sunglasses and a beret low on his forehead, watched the ancient ritual on one of the jumbo screens in Saint Peter's Square. The whole spectacle, the oaths of loyalty and obedience, the professions of faith, the pope's pious exhortation, made him feel edgy. Grotti watched with a sniper's eye as his boss received his cardinal's biretta. Then, his assigned target, Charles Cullen, knelt before the pope to receive his red hat. Earlier, Grotti had tried without success to spot Bryn Martin among the assembled bishops. No matter. *Rest easy, paisan. Your time hasn't come. Not yet.*

"There! I think I see him!" Martin said to Tosco, holding a head shot of Grotti up toward one screen. "Standing next to one of Bernini's columns on the south side of the square. He's dressed as a priest. Sunglasses. Wearing a beret."

Tosco was already talking to the Carabinieri captain in the plaza when Martin said, "I've lost him. He must have stepped behind one of the columns." Both men scrutinized the screen. The crowd was beginning to mill about now that the consistory was almost over. The screen showed carabinieri picking their way quickly through the crowd to the area where Grotti had just stood, stopping a few bereted priests as they went.

"Close off the square," Tosco yelled into the mic attached to his headset. "If we're quick enough, we'll have Grotti trapped. I want a check point at every exit."

Martin nodded.

"*Andiamo!*" Tosco said.

The two raced together out the door of the command center.

Minutes later they stood, panting, quizzing the Carabinieri captain in the area of the square where Martin had spotted Grotti. The crowd seemed restive about having to queue up in order to exit the square. Those inside the basilica, sensing something had happened, exchanged troubled looks when they were ordered to remain inside.

Half an hour later, with the square empty but for gendarmes and carabinieri, Tosco and Martin stood frustrated. There was no sign of Grotti.

"I felt sure the man I saw was Grotti. Maybe I was mistaken."

Tosco frowned. "You did the right thing, Bishop. You've got to go with your gut, what you see…what you think you see."

They turned to see the Carabinieri captain running up to them holding what at first looked like a black coat. "We found this cassock, Inspector, behind one of the columns."

Martin shook his head. "It was a double disguise." He looked at the uniforms swarming the square. "I'll bet you my First Communion money that Grotti was wearing a carabiniere's uniform under this cassock."

26

"Not a word," the newly minted Cardinal, Charles Cullen, reported to Bishop Bryn Martin. "Not one word! Montaldo and I didn't speak at all before, during, or after the consistory. Not even eye contact. It was eerie, Bryn, really eerie."

The two friends had found a private corner in the Aula Paolo VI, where Cullen and eight of the other new cardinals would soon host their *visite di cortesia*. The other four cardinals, including Montaldo, would receive their friends and families within the frescoed walls of the Sala Regia and the Sala Ducale, adjacent chambers in the Apostolic Palace.

"You saw Grotti in the square?" Cullen said. "I wonder what that was all about?"

"I don't know."

"Maybe it was just to rattle us."

Martin quickly corrected the notion, "Probably not, Charles. Grotti can't know that we've been warned. No, he wasn't there to rattle our nerves. He came to size up our security."

"Yeah," Cullen said thoughtfully, "that makes more sense."

"But, Charles, I mean, *Your Eminence*," Martin said with a genuine smile, "right now just enjoy the congratulations about to come your way."

Cullen moved to take his assigned place in the Aula Paolo VI, with Paolo Corsi still at his side, still in his black cassock. The secretary's role was to hand each of the well-wishers a memento card with a picture of the new cardinal.

Cardinal Cullen glanced to where Nora, Ian, Ella, and Margaret were standing. They knew they would have time with the new cardinal back at the hotel, so they hadn't queued up. The ever-generous Merrimans had hired a licensed Vatican photographer to capture each of the hundreds of well-wishers as they congratulated the new Cardinal Archbishop of Baltimore.

"This could go on for hours," Margaret said, looking a bit tired. Ella and the others smiled in agreement.

Nora and Ian moved a few steps away from the others. "This *visite di cortesia* makes me uncomfortable," Nora said in almost a whisper.

"Me, too. Charles is more vulnerable here than he was at the consistory…or will be at the Mass tomorrow."

Ian and Nora scanned the long line of smiling well-wishers inching forward, eager to shake the hand of the ecclesial equivalent of a rock star. They spotted three giggling teenage girls posing for selfies next to a Swiss Guard in his gaudy striped blue, red, orange, and yellow uniform, the guard struggling mightily not to smile. The Merrimans, among the first to congratulate Cullen, moved about chatting with people they knew in the Baltimore contingent.

"It reminds me," Nora said, "of a wedding reception just before the guests sit down to dinner."

"With a few dismaying differences," Ian lamented. "No food, no drink, no open bar!"

In the back of the cavernous hall, Bryn Martin stood with Lorenzo Tosco. Both men had their eyes on the long line inching toward the new Cardinal Archbishop of Baltimore. Without taking his eyes off the sea of well-wishers, Martin asked, "You employ about 140 officers, Inspector?"

"Almost 150. And twenty-four of the gendarmes have had special training in counterterrorism. Half of those are here in the Aula this evening. All of them will be working the Pontifical Mass tomorrow."

Martin nodded as if to say, *Impressive.*

Tosco continued, "We have over a thousand surveillance cameras in place throughout the Vatican. But Grotti has been able to move about with impunity in spite of them."

"His window of opportunity is shrinking," Martin said. "We seem to have made it through today. I hope we can say the same tomorrow and Monday."

Cardinals Alessandro Oradini and Andrea Vannucci settled into two chairs along the side wall of the Sala Regia, the Royal Room, a magnificent, barrel-vaulted Renaissance antechamber to the Sistine Chapel. Their presence was their grudging tribute to Montaldo. They would escape as soon as they could. In the meantime, they would watch with indifference a line of well-wishers moving slowly toward his Eminence, Cardinal Pietro Montaldo. Now in simple black cassocks, adorned only by their episcopal crosses and the scarlet zucchettos on the crest of their skulls, they sat like two old men attending a wake.

Oradini whispered to Vannucci, "There's the American leader of the Brotherhood of the Sacred Purple."

"Yes, I see him. Monsignor Kempe, accompanied no doubt by a few Baltimore priests who have chosen to honor their secret leader in lieu of their own archbishop."

Oradini remained stone-faced. "And look at the glamour boy, Father Trace Dunmore, flirting with the English-speaking seminarians," Oradini hissed. "There is our future."

Annoyed by the fuss of photographers and the studied smiles of diplomatic politeness on the faces of Montaldo's fawning cadre, Oradini thought it was time to make a quiet exit. Before he could rise, Vanucci placed a hand on his arm.

"Our brother cardinal has two major challenges facing him." Oradini gave Vanucci a sidelong glance and waited for him to go on. "He has to keep his secret societies secret. That's not going to be easy. Some embers may be ready to re-ignite in Baltimore and Cleveland. Pietro is right—Cullen and Martin know too much. They threaten our whole movement."

"And...?" Oradini said.

"Pietro, of course, wants to be the leader of the Vatican's staunch right guard. He has the cunning, the money, and the network, but he doesn't have nearly as many of the curia with him as he believes. Moreover, he's up in Perugia." He raised an eyebrow. "Distance makes a difference."

"All true," Oradini agreed. "But he knows all the secrets—including our own. And he knows how to capitalize on the power those secrets give him."

"Yes. In this game, Pietro Montaldo is the undisputed master. He knows the rules, and knows even better how to break them."

The two old cardinals, veterans of ecclesiastical intrigue, sat in silence, indifferent to the Sala Regia's overpowering baroque frescoes and intricately inlaid marble floors.

Oradini added, "I hope we haven't made a mistake in abetting Montaldo's rise in the papal court."

Vannucci broke in, "And at no inconsiderable personal expense!"

"And with what to show for it?" Oradini added ruefully as both men rose wearily and slipped quietly out of the Sala Regia.

Monsignor Aidan Kempe, having completed his duties as Cardinal Montaldo's secretary for the consistory, stood against one wall of the Sala Regia with Fathers Tom Fenton and Herm Volker. When their turn had come to greet the cardinal, Fenton and

Volker had hoped he would have given them some recognition as Brothers of the Sacred Purple. The received no such acknowledgment. Like grade-school boys not getting a single Valentine, they were hurt.

"I need a drink," Fenton said, shoving Montaldo's folded memento card into his suitcoat pocket. "Why hang around here?"

Kempe didn't hear a word he said. Right before his eyes, just inside the Sala Regia with a few others in Cullen's party, was Margaret Comiskey. *Why in God's name had Cullen invited her?* Comiskey had been his secretary when he was the chief financial officer of the archdiocese. She was the witch who ran to Martin and Cullen with accusations that he was stealing.

"What did you say, Tom?" he asked, coming back into the moment with the two priests. "I was distracted by that Comiskey woman." His companions followed his glare. "Standing near the entrance, gawking at the frescos like a tourist. The one in blue."

"I was suggesting we head out for a stiff drink."

"An excellent idea. Come on." Kempe marched straight toward Comiskey with Fenton and Volker a step behind, like a mismatched pair of bodyguards.

Margaret didn't notice him until he was a few steps away. Kempe stopped inches in front of Margaret and spat out a single word, "Traitor!" and then marched off with Fenton and Volker in tow. Ella Landers guided her shaken friend to some chairs lined up against one wall of the Sala. Ian and Nora, a few steps away, noticed the altercation and followed them.

Ian shook his head in dismay at Kempe's rudeness. "I shouldn't have suggested we come over here. But the Sala Regia and Sala Ducale are so seldom open to the public I thought it would be a shame to miss the opportunity to visit both."

"Not at all, Ian," Margaret said with a steady voice. "I've known the kind of man Aidan Kempe is for a long time. This just confirms…" Comiskey left her sentence unfinished and looked up. Montaldo was still mingling with the fifty or so guests who were slow to leave the reception, giving his photographer ample opportunity for informal shots. "Let's just mingle a bit and enjoy these exquisite rooms."

"Yes," Nora said with a sly smile, "and I'd like to get a closer look at Pietro Montaldo, the grand master of secret societies."

27

There was nothing that really surprised Grotti in the security plan for the consistory. In addition to being cognizant of the usual heightened security procedures by Vatican and Roman police on duty, he knew he had to pay careful attention to the enhanced technological tools at their disposal. *You can never be sure*, he warned himself, *that you are not on camera.* Grotti smiled wearily. His night of soul searching had borne fruit. And soon he would have in hand the potion he needed to execute his plan. Vittoria Massi was still working at the hospital and wouldn't return to the apartment for another four hours. Time he needed for sleep. He went to her window, parted the curtain a few inches, and peered out. When he was on assignment, he always assumed active surveillance might be in place. But since the close call in Saint Peter's Square, he also suspected he was being actively hunted. The gendarmes in the square had stopped and questioned a few men in clerical dress who roughly fit his own description. This made his endeavor all the more challenging. And Giorgio Grotti had another score to settle. Angelo Correa, his partner in the enterprise, had betrayed him. He numbered the people who knew about his assignment: Montaldo, Correa, his don, and, of course, Vittoria. On the narrow street below Vittoria's apartment everything seemed normal. Two waddling old women with baskets over their arms on their way to the market, a silver Vespa leaning against a wall, somewhere the forlorn yowling of a cat. Grotti dropped the curtain back in place.

Ten minutes later the cardinal's assassin was asleep.

Cardinal Charles Cullen, dressed in a white collarless shirt and black trousers, sat with his inner circle of confidants—Bryn Martin, Ian, and Nora—in his suite at the Raphael. His cardinal's robes hung on a regally emblazoned Mancinelli hanger in the suite's closet next to his cotton flannel pajamas.

"How are you holding up, Charles?" Martin asked.

"Exhausted. But as relaxed as circumstances allow," Cullen answered. "Above all else," he glanced around the room at his friends, "happy. Happy and grateful. So far, so good." An empty bottle of champagne lay canted in an ice bucket on the coffee table next to a picked-over tray of cheeses, crackers, salami, and olives.

"Montaldo and I ignored each other. As if we didn't exist to each other. Even after we were paired together."

Ian smiled. "Doesn't 'consistory' mean to stand shoulder to shoulder? To stand together. What an irony!"

Cullen shook his head. "Yeah. Two people standing together while one orders the assassination of the other."

"The church has a long history of using a consistory or conclave as a locus for all kinds of treachery. Blackmail, bribery... and the murder most foul of cardinals and popes," Ian added.

"That calls to mind the kiss of peace at the Papal Mass tomorrow. Pietro Montaldo and I will exchange the *Pax Tecum!*" Cullen said with a shudder.

Nora broke the heaviness in the room. "We understand, Charles. Even a handshake should be real, should be sincere. Otherwise it's a lie. Or a betrayal."

Ian reached for Nora's hand.

Then Cullen said haltingly, "What galls me is the duplicity of it all. Like two Mafia godfathers embracing as they plot each other's murder. I'd prefer to have no part in it."

Nora patted Cullen's hand.

"I'll be praying during the Mass," Cullen said with his eyes lowered, "for the freedom and grace of humility. Let's hope my prayer does not go unanswered."

28

At the next morning's papal Mass, Nora, Ian, Ella, and Margaret once again found themselves seated in the left transept of the basilica. They were as close to the high altar—and the pope and new cardinals—as members of the laity could get. The large sanctuary area in front of the altar held two banks of cardinal concelebrants, while at the front of the central nave stood a phalanx of bishops and priests vested in green chasubles. It was at this Mass following the consistory that the new cardinals were to receive their cardinal's ring and a parchment inscribed with the seal and signature of the pope, confirming their rights and privileges as a titular head of one of Rome's churches.

Martin sat between a smiling bishop from Tanzania and a German bishop whose English was not as good as the man thought it was. Thankfully, their conversation was brief. Martin's attention went back and forth from Cullen and Montaldo to the Swiss Guard. Everything looked good. He'd had only a quick word with Inspector Lorenzo Tosco before the lengthy processional. Tosco reported nothing unusual or suspicious.

After the homily, the entire assembly sat briefly in silence. When the pontiff rose, the master of ceremonies beckoned the new cardinals to come forward in single file to receive their rings.

Margaret glanced at her booklet for the translation of the words he spoke. "Receive the ring from the hand of Peter and know that your love for the church is strengthened by the love of the Prince of the Apostles." She read with interest a note describing the ring: "The modernist design depicts the crucifixion with Mary and St. John portrayed at the foot of the cross." Upon receiving his ring, each new cardinal would exchange the kiss of peace with the pope and then move slowly among the other new members of the college exchanging the *Pax.*

Nora stood on her toes, straining to see the actual kiss of peace between Charles Cullen and Pietro Montaldo.

"Did you see that?" she asked Ian. "Charles must have said something to Montaldo."

"I wonder what."

"It seemed to rattle Montaldo," Nora added.

The new cardinals moved in line to the rows of their seniors in the college to exchange the kiss of peace. As the line of newly minted cardinals began to inch their way down each row of the assembled cardinals, the pontifical choir intoned a lilting hymn that seemed by its tempo to be urging the cardinals to get on with it, a song that would be repeated for as long as the ancient rite lasted.

"It's choreographed, like a high church *pas de deux,*" Ella said, leaning toward Margaret. "Look, two cardinals face each other, they take a half step forward with their right foot, then with their left cheek, touch the other's left cheek, then it's right cheek to right cheek."

"Yes," Margaret said under her breath, "I see what you mean. Then after they say whatever they say… 'Pax Tecum,' or 'Peace be with you,' or simply 'Christ's peace,' they take a sidestep to the next cardinal." *A kind of a liturgical do-si-do,* she thought.

Nora and Ian strained, without success, to hear what the two women were whispering about that seemed so amusing.

Ella turned serious. "Most of the cardinals, I assume, know one another or at least know *of* one another. Don't you think?"

Margaret nodded. "With more than a few exceptions. The Roman Catholic Church is a pretty big tent."

"Some are friends. I guess," Ella said as she and Margaret watched Cardinal Cullen move from cardinal to cardinal exchanging a gesture of fraternal love and communion in Christ. "And some are enemies."

29

The best time to strike, Grotti had determined, would be very late in the evening, just before the new Prince of the Church was preparing to retire after one of the most significant days of his life. The hotel's security would be but a minor challenge for this former carabiniere. Access to the suite had already been arranged, and the service elevator he had selected as his exit route would deliver him just a few steps from the hotel's 24-hour loading dock. His Eminence would be tired from the long ceremony, the greeting of well-wishers, the elegant meal, and the flattering after-dinner speeches. *And his defenses will be down.*

After the long Pontifical Mass, Margaret Comiskey and Ella Landers were much in need of an afternoon nap and couldn't wait to get back to their room and kick their shoes off. But while they were all waiting for an elevator car, Cardinal Cullen asked a favor that would keep the two women occupied for a while.

"There are two reporters here from the *Baltimore Sun*," the cardinal said. "A man and a woman, I think. They've been after me for an interview and left contact information at the registration desk. If you can reach them, would you invite them to the dinner this evening?"

"Of course, Your Eminence" Margaret said, giggling almost imperceptibly at finding herself using Cullen's formal title.

As the elevator doors opened, Cullen thought of another errand. "The School Sisters of Notre Dame in Baltimore have two members on their Congregation's General Council in Rome. Let's invite them to dinner as well." Almost as an afterthought he added, "And any other stray Baltimoreans you might find who came to the consistory on their own dime."

Bryn Martin, alone in his hotel room, sat in an overstuffed easy chair with his feet up on the chair's ottoman, talking on his cell with Inspector Tosco. "Giorgio's window is closing, Inspector. I don't know if that's a good thing or not."

Tosco let the remark pass. "Paolo Corsi will be covering you and the cardinal to and from La Campana this evening. And I'll be close by with a plainclothes female gendarme accompanying me. Just a bit more security. So there will be two of us inside the restaurant, with Corsi and others outside, including, if I can arrange it, a few plain-clothes carabinieri. They will definitely keep an eye on the kitchen entrance."

"Cardinal Cullen and I are very grateful, Inspector. You and your gendarmes have really eased our anxiety."

"You are very welcome, Bishop. I will see you this evening, then. Ciao."

Martin longed to pull the drapes and stretch out on his bed. But first, he had one more call to make.

30

Charles Cullen stood at the entrance to the private dining room reserved for his guests at La Compana. He was dressed in a Mancinelli-tailored cassock and *mozzetta*— the mini-cape that reached only to the elbows—both trimmed in the scarlet piping of a cardinal.

Bryn Martin, in a black suit with a pendant pectoral cross, stood next to him, scanning the twelve tables, each decorated with a floral centerpiece, each with lighted tapers in flutes, and carafes of red and white wines. "It looks like we're ready for quite a party, Charles."

"Thanks for taking care of the seating assignments."

"It was mostly the work of our lady friends," Martin confessed. "They have you seated with the Merrimans and two other couples from the Catholic Charities board. I'm with Nora, Ian, Margaret, Ella, and Ian's friend, Tom Hathaway. They've left most of the other tables unassigned. It should be fun."

"Yes," Cullen said warily, "it *should* be fun, *shouldn't* it?"

Twenty minutes later, with most of the guests seated, Martin tapped his water glass with a fork.

"Cardinal Cullen has asked me to say grace. But before I do that, may I ask you to stand and join me in applauding the Cardinal Archbishop of Baltimore, Charles Cullen!" The warm round of cheers that followed was strong and sustained, prompting a red-faced Cullen to finally rise and wave it down.

"Let's be still for just a moment," Bishop Martin said then. As the room quieted, he began, "Dear God, we gather with joyful hearts to ask your blessing on this meal, on this gathering of your servants. We especially ask your blessing on your faithful servant, Cardinal Charles Cullen. Bless his leadership of the church in Baltimore, and now bless his service to our Holy Father and our universal Catholic Church as a member of the College of Cardinals. We thank you for sustaining with your love this shepherd-servant, whom we have all come to know and love. As we ask for your blessing, we lift up to your loving compassion those who hunger for bread, for shelter, for justice, for peace. We pray in the name of the Father, Son, and Holy Spirit. Amen."

With that, the servers moved out from the kitchen with trays of Italian wedding soup, soon to be followed by linguine with clam sauce, and an entree of chicken parmigiana. The feast had begun.

By the time Martin had moved back to his chair, Ian had introduced his university friend Tom Hathaway to the rest of the table. "Tom and I met at Oxford many years ago. And my friendship with this very serious and very joyful and wickedly funny man was a factor that had me thinking about joining the Dominicans. But that's another story."

Ian stole a quick glance at Nora.

"Well, our loss is your gain," Tom said to Nora.

Nora colored slightly and quickly changed the subject. "Ian mentioned you teach both seminarians and grad school priests at the Angelicum, Tom. And lay people—even women!"

"I don't know how I could stand it if it were all men," Tom said. "It's not healthy, for me or the seminarians. Without the participation of women, the politics in our church would be so much worse than they are right now. Most of the faculty are friends, but I'm afraid that at the Angelicum we're dealing with the same extreme polarization we find everywhere in the church and, I guess, society at large."

Margaret added, "That polarization has pretty deeply divided the College of Cardinals into pre-Vatican and post-Vatican factions."

"Father Hathaway," Ella asked, "aren't today's divisions much the same as Catholics have known since the Enlightenment? Or is this something different?"

"Your son and I wrestled with that question years ago at Oxford," Hathaway said tentatively. "The discussion continues. I think we are witnessing a far more complex polarization today. There are different levels to the division. Theological, sociological, cultural, even issues of communal identity are all at play here. How you feel about a single issue defines whose side you are on."

"And don't leave out the role of power and control," Nora added. "Or our compulsion to blog and tweet and text, or our 24/7 cascade of talking heads on TV."

Bryn broke in on his sister a little brusquely, "If I can add my two cents worth to this significant discussion: Would someone please pass me the red wine?"

With that mild admonishment, the table relaxed a little.

"I read an article of yours, Tom," Bryn said, "I think it was in *Commonweal*. The title caught me: 'Loose in the World.' You wrote, if my memory is correct, that the Catholic Church doesn't have a lock on the Holy Spirit. And don't we act as if we do believe that sometimes? Maybe most of the time. It's as if we maintain that the Holy Spirit works mainly through the church's sacraments and through its bishops to enlighten and heal and direct God's holy people. But you are on to something. The Holy Spirit really is loose in the world, free to move where she will through all of God's creatures."

"I'm happy to know you read it, Bryn, and got it, and honored that you remember it. That was the main idea I wanted to get across. The wisdom of the Spirit dwells on both sides of our polarized church."

"Oh, that's interesting!" Margaret said. "If we all took your point more seriously, it might actually bring a note of civility to our screeds across the current divide. We can be so mean in our righteous defense of our own cherished tenets."

"And sometimes we're not only mean, Margaret," Bryn said. "Sometimes we're violent. Nora and Ian have heard this Blaise Pascal quote from me a number of times, but they're going to hear it again: 'Men never do evil so completely and cheerfully as when they do it from religious conviction.'"

A sudden, thoughtful, silence fell on the table. Before anyone could react to Pascal's insight, the pasta plates were cleared in preparation for the serving of the main course.

Between courses, Charles Cullen moved from table to table greeting each of his guests. He gave a warm hug to two School Sisters of Notre Dame, who expressed their delight at being included in the dinner. When he passed Lorenzo Tosco's table, he caught a nod from the Inspector that said everything was in order. No sign of trouble. The *Baltimore Sun* reporters at another table confirmed their breakfast interview with him at 8:00 the next morning. Their stories on the consistory had been filed and would appear in the Sunday edition of the *Sun*. Their interview with him would appear in a few days, they told him.

Before Cullen could return to his table, Martin appeared at his side and whispered, "There's someone in the bar I'd like you to meet."

Cullen followed Martin to the bar, not sure what to expect. A well-dressed man rose from a corner table and approached the new cardinal.

"Cardinal Cullen," Martin said formally, "I'd like you to meet

Don Leonine Scarano. Mr. Scarano, Cardinal Cullen."

A thoroughly surprised cardinal flashed a quick glance at Martin.

"It's a great privilege to meet you, *Eminenza*," Scarano said, kissing the cardinal's new ring.

"The privilege is mine," Cullen said. "I am happy to have a chance to thank you personally for what you have done for Bishop Martin and me."

Scarano shrugged. "You are very welcome, *Eminenza*." The don hesitated. "I had a very interesting conversation the other night with Bishop Martin. Perhaps he told you about it. These are such difficult times for our church."

"Yes, he did. And yes, they are indeed difficult, and dangerous, times."

Turning to Martin, Scarano said, "Please tell my cousins in Cleveland, especially Sister Amelia, that I send them my love."

The little scene had captured the attention of the bartender and patrons at the bar.

"I should get back to my guests, Mr. Scarano," Cullen said. "Thank you for all you've done. God bless you."

Cullen and Martin walked slowly back into the dining room. "That was very thoughtful of you, Bryn. Thank you, thank you."

31

Giorgio Grotti unzipped a small, black toiletry kit to make sure he had everything he might need for the grim task ahead. It was all there—a vial of chloroform, a cloth to apply it, a 15-cc vial of potassium chloride, and a syringe with an 18-gauge needle. *Thank you, Vittoria.* He looked at his watch. Cardinal Cullen would be at his dinner at the La Compana by now, with flanks of security personnel both inside and outside the restaurant. *As if that could have stopped me. Go ahead and enjoy your little party, Eminenza.*

Monsignor Kempe and Fathers Fenton and Volker were seated at a round table with three minor officials, all priests, all associates of their movement now working in the Vatican. The five-star La Pergola Restaurant, located in the five-star Cavalieri Hotel, had been chosen for the banquet by Cardinal Montaldo himself. He was sparing no expense in celebrating his elevation to the College of Cardinals. The elegant, chandeliered dining room glimmered in the indirect lighting that highlighted the crystal and cutlery at each of the ninety place settings. The color scheme, surprising to some, was not the scarlet red of the cardinal, but rather purple, the color of old royalty. The napkins were freshly ironed purple linen. The flower arrangements at each table included Italian asters, foxgloves, and pansies in shades from lavender to violet. And at each setting was placed a gift from the new cardinal—

a set of cufflinks with a purple stone for the men and a set of purple lacquered earrings for the few women present.

Kempe wasn't surprised to observe that the majority of guests were clergy—a half dozen cardinals among them, another two dozen bishops. Many of the priests in the room bore a small fuchsia piping at the base of their white collars signaling their rank of monsignor. The laity were in formal attire, more than a few wearing the sash and insignia of the Knights of Malta.

The Vatican priests at Kempe's table soon discovered that he, Fenton, and Volker were mere parish priests, from America no less, and turned to closed conversations in rapid Italian.

Kempe couldn't help himself. Speaking just loud enough for the Vatican clergy to hear, he said to Fenton and Volker, "His Eminence is flying his true colors this evening." The three priests sitting across from him were suddenly paying attention. "Cardinal Montaldo," Kempe continued, now speaking to the whole table, "had a special regard for the clergy of Baltimore." And after a pause, "We 'chosen ones' made up a special cadre connected to the new Cardinal Archbishop of Perugia called the Brotherhood of the Sacred Purple." Aidan Kempe could tell by their expressions that the three arrogant little bastards, now looking at him intently, really didn't know much, and perhaps knew nothing more than rumors, about the Brotherhood of the Sacred Purple.

"May I have your attention, please," Father Trace Dunmore said, standing at the head table with a portable microphone in his hand. "I know I speak for all of us here in giving thanks to Almighty God for raising the Archbishop of Perugia, Pietro Montaldo, to the College of Cardinals." There followed a polite spattering of applause. I now ask His Eminence, Cardinal Andrea Oradini, to lead us in the benediction."

The old cardinal, his hands pressing the table for leverage, rose slowly as Father Dunmore handed him the mic. "Please remain seated for the blessing," Oradini said, clearing his throat and letting a few seconds tick past. "Almighty God, we gather in the name of Jesus, Our Savior, to ask your blessing on your faithful bishop, Pietro Gonzaga Montaldo, now *Car-din-al-e* of your most holy Catholic Church. Sustain him with your strength and wisdom to fight the enemies of your holy church, both within and without. May he bring the glory and truth of the Roman Catholic faith to the corners of our secular and vainglorious world. May the intercession of Saint Peter and Saint Aloysius Gonzaga give him strength. And may our Blessed Mother, the Holy Virgin, give him comfort. Bless now with your holy presence this banquet of thanksgiving and praise. In the name of the Father, the Son, and the Holy Spirit. Amen."

An hour later, when an elaborate presentation was made of the main course, veal saltimbocca, Monsignor Aidan Kempe enjoyed complete command of his table.

32

The bored carabiniere on lobby duty at the Raphael Hotel glanced at her watch. 10:00 p.m. Almost two more hours until her shift ended. She looked up from her magazine a moment later as two habited nuns crossed with purposeful strides toward the registration desk. Something about them didn't seem quite right. And it was awfully late in the evening for vowed religious women to be out and about in Rome.

Both were dressed in ankle-length gray skirts and gray cotton blouses, and both wore black veils over starched white wimples that together shrouded their foreheads and cheeks. One had to be close to six feet tall. The one who seemed to be in charge was somewhat shorter. Maybe five eight or five nine. Both were slim, almost athletic.

The clerk on duty looked up at the approach of two nuns. "May I help you, Sister?" she asked, speaking to the shorter of the two. She was a not unattractive woman, and a little hard-looking for a nun.

"We're here to deliver messages from our Provincial Superior, Mother Agnes, for Cardinal Cullen and Bishop Martin, two of your guests."

"They're not here at present, Sister. Cardinal Cullen and his group went out for dinner. I don't know when they will return."

"Yes, we understood that they would be," said the shorter

nun. She took two envelopes from the folds of her habit and placed them on the mahogany counter. Sliding them toward the clerk, she said, "Please deliver these messages…not tonight… but tomorrow morning. Mother Agnes was very specific on that point. They contain some sad news, and Mother Agnes doesn't want to spoil the cardinal's special day. It's very important that you hold them until tomorrow."

The clerk hesitated for a second, then said, "Of course, Sister, we'll see they're delivered tomorrow morning."

The nun who had given her the notes said pleasantly, "Thank you very much. Good evening."

The carabiniere watched as the two nuns turned and walked out of the hotel, the tall one plodding with a heavy step. The cop rose from her chair and walked across the lobby to the desk. Showing her badge she asked the clerk casually, "What was that all about?"

The clerk shrugged and said, "They were delivering messages for two guests of the hotel."

"May I see them?"

It wasn't really a question, but the clerk demurred. "I'm afraid that would be against hotel policy."

The carabiniere tried to read the writing on the face of the top envelope, in a somewhat feminine script, but the clerk snatched them away.

"If you want to read them so badly, go wake up a judge."

The carabiniere stood at the counter for a few seconds, offering the clerk a hard look, but turned at last and went back to her magazine.

33

It was a wonderful dinner, Charles, thank you," Nora said wearily. Bryn, Nora, and Ian were once again gathered in the cardinal's suite to review the security measures for tomorrow, their final full day in the Eternal City.

"Your welcome, Nora. But thanks properly go to the Merrimans and a few other generous families for underwriting this long weekend in Rome. Maybe tomorrow we can all take it easy. We haven't had any time to really relax. The only thing I have scheduled is a breakfast meeting with the *Sun* reporters."

"Tosco will have a few of his people tagging along if Charles or I leave the hotel," Martin said, stifling a yawn. "There will be a plainclothes carabiniere here at the hotel through the night. But he wasn't sure about tomorrow."

"But Giorgio Grotti is still out there," Ian said, expecting it was what they were all thinking.

The energy level in the room was ebbing steadily.

"It's late, Charles, and we're all tired," Nora said gently, "but Ian and I saw Montaldo react when you whispered something to him during the Kiss of Peace. Is it something you can share with us?"

Cullen felt himself coloring. "You may remember that I said I wasn't comfortable with the thought of giving the *Pax* to Montaldo." A wisp of a smile rose to his lips. "My pride got the best of me, I'm afraid. It really did. I hissed a single word into his ear: 'Cain!'" Cullen's three friends fell silent. "I'll never forget

139

the look in his eyes. He was stunned, baffled, angered...all those things. I confess that I found myself relishing his sudden shock in learning that I know about his plot."

Martin broke the silence that followed. "Maybe the realization that you know what he is up to will force a change in plans. He might feel that *he's* now the one in jeopardy."

"That's possible," Cullen said. "But I still don't feel good about what I did."

"You both need to be especially careful tomorrow," Nora said looking intently at each of them. "It's no time to let your guard down."

The Cardinal Archbishop of Baltimore smiled. "Let's just try to make it through the night."

34

Timing, Grotti knew, was critical. And he thought of himself as a master of timing. So he would wait, wait as long as it took, for the door to open to the new cardinal's suite. He wanted it to appear that he was just about to knock. And his patience paid off.

Well after eleven o'clock, the door opened as Father Trace Dunmore and Simon Ashley exited Montaldo's suite. There, with his fist raised to knock, stood Giorgio Grotti.

"Grotti," Ashley said, surprised to see him, "What are you doing here?"

"I'm here to make a report to Cardinal Montaldo. A report for his ears only. So, if you two would please give us some privacy."

Grotti brushed past them, into the suite, and closed the door in their faces. Then he slipped the deadbolt closed.

Cardinal Pietro Montaldo glanced up without much expression. He looked exhausted.

"So, Giorgio? Is it done? Be brief. It's been a long day and I'm dying to get to bed."

"Of course, *Eminenza*, I won't tire you much further. This will take only a moment."

35

Rome's media outlets raced to break the news that a cardinal just elevated by the pope had been found dead in his suite at the Cavalieri Hotel. The Archbishop of Perugia, Pietro Gonzaga Montaldo, just two days earlier raised to the dignity of Cardinal of the Roman Catholic Church, was dead, apparently of natural causes. Cardinals are for the most part older men, and the death of a member of the hierarchy is not uncommon, but the timing in this case made some journalists skeptical. More than a few were speculating that there might be more to the story.

Bryn Martin, still in his pajamas, was on the phone with Lorenzo Tosco.

"What do you make of this, Inspector?"

"The Carabinieri are investigating. Rather feverishly, I might add. My contact there said there are no signs of foul play. No forced entry, no physical signs of assault. For the moment, it seems Cardinal Montaldo's died a natural death. Perhaps a stroke or heart attack."

"I need to get dressed and go over to Cardinal Cullen's suite. I'm still concerned about Giorgio Grotti."

"Of course. I am too. I'll be at the Raphael around eleven this morning. Can you gather the cardinal, and those close to him, in his suite? I should have more information then."

"Yes, that would be very helpful, Inspector. We'll be there at eleven."

Martin pressed Cullen's speed-dial button. No answer. Then he remembered that the cardinal had agreed to a breakfast meeting with two *Sun* reporters. He must be in the dining room or lobby. Minutes later, Martin, his breathing shallow and rapid, stood waiting for an elevator. When the doors slid open, Nora and Ian were in the elevator car.

"Thank God, you're all right, Bryn," Nora said. "We just heard about Montaldo."

"I'm fine. But I need to talk to Charles. He should be meeting with the reporters from the *Sun*."

"He is," Ian said. "They're in the dining room. I went down earlier for coffee and they were wrapped in discussion. Montaldo's death is all over the news. Charles has to be so distracted."

Just as Ian had reported, Cardinal Cullen was seated at breakfast with the *Sun* reporters when Martin, Nora, and Ian came into the dining room.

"I'll join you in a minute. Get a table, would you?" Martin said, and walked over to Cullen's table. "Excuse me," he said to the reporters, "but I need just a word with Cardinal Cullen."

Cullen and Martin walked into the lobby and found a quiet corner.

"Montaldo was found dead in his hotel room this morning. No sign of foul play."

"Good Lord! I'm stunned."

"Me, too, Charles. But we need to stay focused. Grotti is still out there somewhere and we need to be careful, very careful."

"I know," is all Cullen could manage to say.

"I just spoke with Tosco. He wants to meet with us—you, me, Nora, and Ian—at eleven, in your suite. Maybe he'll have additional information on Montaldo's death, and maybe even on Grotti's whereabouts."

"What a strange turn, Bryn. For God's sake! What's going on?"

"I have no idea. But I think we need to kick this upstairs. Someone in the curia needs to know about our suspicions."

Cullen glowered, but said, "I'll make the call."

Shortly after Lorenzo Tosco arrived in Cullen's suite, he was introduced to Margaret Comiskey and Ella Martin.

"I've asked Margaret and Ella to join us, Inspector. Ian has made them both aware of the warning Bryn and I received from Leonine Scarano. They are both familiar with the priests Cardinal Montaldo had working as his agents in Baltimore. Margaret, in fact, once had a threatening encounter with Giorgio Grotti. She can tell you about that later if you think it would help. But of all of us here, she's the only one who has seen him up close."

Tosco nodded. "Yes, I would like to hear about your incident with Grotti. Perhaps after I tell you what I've heard from the Carabinieri this morning. At first glance, Cardinal Montaldo's death appears to be from natural causes. The medical examiner's report will be released to me soon. Maybe even before you leave. As I recall, you're scheduled to fly out tomorrow morning."

"Around 10:30," Cullen confirmed.

"You're not staying for Montaldo's funeral, then?" Martin asked.

"No. I don't want to stay here any longer than necessary."

"We are newly aware," Tosco said, "that Cardinal Montaldo had a dark side to his life. But much of that dark side wasn't as secret as he thought. The Carabinieri have heard the rumors making their way through the halls of the Vatican and among Rome's movers and shakers. So, the police investigating his death are going to be especially careful. But for now, his death, in the words of the Vatican Press Office, is 'a shocking personal tragedy.'"

Martin asked, "Who was the last person to see Montaldo alive?"

"Father Trace Dunmore and Simon Ashley, two aides to the cardinal, told the Carabinieri that they left his suite around eleven. They said the cardinal looked fine to them but was very tired from the Papal Mass and a long celebratory banquet with too many toasts and tributes. And they mentioned that Cardinal Montaldo had just taken his blood pressure medication. The Carabinieri have their full statement, but that's the substance of it."

No one spoke as they looked at one another with concern… and anxiety.

Before Tosco could go on, there was a knock on the door. Ian answered to find a young woman from the hotel staff.

"I received a message for the cardinal at the start of my shift last night that we were asked to deliver this morning." She looked into the room and saw Bishop Martin. "And one for you, too, Bishop. They were dropped off by two nuns." She stepped into the room and handed each man an envelope with his name on it. She turned to leave but Tosco signaled for her to wait with a raised index finger.

Cullen and Martin sat looking at the envelopes in their hands. Then, carefully, they opened them, taking a single sheet of paper from each. They took but a second to read and the two men exchanged a quizzical look.

Cullen spoke first. "Just three words in Latin: *Vade in pace.* 'Go in peace.'"

"My note says the very same. *Vade in pace.* No salutation. No signature. The message is printed, not in script."

"You received these yourself?" Tosco asked the clerk.

"Yes," the desk clerk said. "I double Sunday nights. The nun who carried the envelopes said the messages were from her superior, a Sister Agnes."

"Nuns you say," Ian offered dubiously.

"They did seem a little odd," the clerk said. "One of them was quite tall, and never spoke, and the other looked…I don't know. Not like a nun."

"How do you mean?" Tosco asked. "They were in religious habits, no?"

The clerk shrugged. "What kind of nun tweezes her eyebrows?"

"It's as if they wanted you to read their cryptic message, *Go in peace*, only after you heard of Montaldo's death," the Inspector said.

"What did the tall one look like?" Ian asked.

"She stood back. But she was very tall, easily six feet. I didn't really get a good look at her face."

"More likely *his* face," Ian said, glancing around the room.

Tosco nodded. "That disguise would be quite like Grotti."

He dismissed the clerk.

Cullen frowned. "Is this message—assuming it's from Grotti —is this message saying in effect that his assignment to assassinate us has been called off? That we can relax? And go home in peace?"

He looked to Tosco.

"That's possible, Cardinal. I agree with Ian that Grotti was likely the taller of the two 'nuns.' As a former seminarian he has some Latin. Let's assume that Grotti, for some reason we don't know, has decided not to go ahead with his assignment to kill you and Bishop Martin. He must have discovered somehow that you knew you were in his sights."

"I all but directly accused Montaldo at the *Pax Tecum!*"

"Perhaps he called Grotti off," Tosco speculated. "He in turn decided to ease your minds by sending his 'Go home in peace' notes. Now that's possible, but it is quite a *stretch* as you say in America! I urge you both to remain vigilant until you all are safe-

146

ly boarded on your plane tomorrow."

"But why, to stay with this theory for a bit, why would Grotti change his mind?" Ian asked.

"Good question," Nora said, "but let me play the conspiracy theorist and suggest that Grotti didn't just change his mind, but changed his target. We suspect that Grotti dropped the message, intending that you not see it until Montaldo was dead. How could he know that if Montaldo died of natural causes? I think that, for some reason, Grotti turned on his boss, the Cardinal Archbishop of Perugia. I think you will soon learn," she said to Tosco, "that Montaldo was murdered."

"Maybe," Ian said, "but what could prompt Grotti to turn on Montaldo?"

Tosco was paying careful attention. "If the medical examiner's report suggests foul play, the Carabinieri will certainly look into Nora's theory."

"When I met with Leonine Scarano last Friday," Martin said, "he told me that Grotti had asked one of the members of his family to help him with the assassinations. The whole family knows that Montaldo was no saint. Not only because of his shady financial dealings, but also because of his frequent visits to teenage prostitutes. And Scarano said Montaldo was known to hit on seminarians. The mob had nothing but contempt for Montaldo. We also know Grotti abhorred homosexuality. I doubt he could have stuck with Montaldo if he had known previously about that side of his boss. And then, perhaps, he hears all about it from Scarano's own enforcer."

Tosco said, "You'll remember, Bishop Martin, that Grotti's reaction to such behavior has led to violence in the past." He glanced around the room and explained what Martin already knew. "Grotti was in the seminary three years when he attacked a seminarian who came on to him. He put the seminarian in the hospital, and was abruptly expelled. Giorgio abhors gay men.

"His turning on Montaldo is all conjecture, of course," he continued. "But we still need to concentrate on our security protocol for your last day in Rome. Grotti is unpredictable and even if the 'Go in peace' message is really from him, it doesn't mean you can afford to let your guard slip. And we now know Grotti has an accomplice. We need to find the identity of the other nun who delivered these notes. I'll put the Carabinieri on that immediately." Shaking open a clean handkerchief he said, "I'll need those notes, and the envelopes." He took them from Martin and Cullen and folded them up in the handkerchief and dropped them into a side pocket of his suit. "We may find fingerprints or DNA that can help identify her. So it's not just Grotti we have to watch out for. I'll keep Corsi tagging along with you whenever you leave the hotel."

"Inspector Tosco," Margaret Comiskey said after hesitating briefly, "Bishop Martin mentioned that we believe this man, Giorgio Grotti, was in my home in Baltimore. He identified himself as Monsignor Giancarlo Foscari, an investigator for the Vatican. Unwisely, I let him into my house. I'm sure he was there to kill me...to strangle me. As he approached me in my kitchen his cell phone rang. I don't know who called him, but whoever it was saved my life. Right after the call, he looked...I don't know... relieved. I don't think he *wanted* to kill me. I think he was *ordered* to kill me. For some reason, the call revoked the order. This Foscari, or Grotti, muttered a quick apology and ran out of my house. What I'm trying to say is that this assassin doesn't kill for the pleasure of it. Perhaps that doesn't make much difference, but I wanted you to know about it."

"Of course it matters. It helps greatly with our psychological profile. Thank you," Tosco said with a slight bow of his head.

Thinking about that day in her kitchen, Margaret shuddered. "Why don't we just go home before something terrible happens?"

The room was quiet for a moment.

"Are you still satisfied with our security arrangements?" Cullen said to Martin, a little doubtfully.

"We are in good hands, Charles," Martin said, nodding. "Finally, I guess I'm just not a man who is easily pushed around."

Tosco rose to leave. "Well then, to the extent that you can, try to enjoy your last day in Rome."

36

Father Trace Dunmore sat in the dining room of the Hotel Cavalieri across from Simon Ashley, who was holding the latest edition of Rome's daily newspaper, *la Repubblica*. The paper seemed to stir to life in his trembling hands. The headline read, "New cardinal found dead in hotel suite." The subhead was in Latin: *Sic transit gloria mundi*—'So goes the glory of the world.'

"Clever little bastards," Ashley remarked, thinking of the headline editors at *la Repubblica*.

"We need to get back to Perugia, like today," Dunmore whispered over their coffees and croissants. "If the police find out that we didn't tell them of Giorgio's late-night visit to Montaldo's suite, we could be in big trouble."

"We'd be in bigger trouble if we had," snapped Ashley. "No, we did the right thing. And, yes, let's get back to Perugia. Our sinecures, my dear Trace, have come to an abrupt end." Ashley squeezed his eyes shut. "What in God's name came over Grotti? Don't think for a minute that his Eminence, Cardinal Pietro Montaldo, died of natural causes. Giorgio Grotti is now our biggest problem. Unless you know of an assassin we can hire to assassinate the cardinal's assassin."

Dunmore managed an ironic sneer. "If the authorities determine that Montaldo was murdered, and if they find and arrest Grotti, they'll be after us next. They'll know we lied to them. And worse, the police in Cleveland might come after us for our part in the murder of those crazy women priests. Grotti has absolutely no reason not to drag us into this mess. He'll sell us out in a minute to bargain for a shorter sentence. We both know Grotti despises us."

"And we have no friends in Rome," Ashley said. "Don't think for a moment that those bastards Oradini or Vannucci will help us. Believe me, they are two very nervous old men right now."

Across Rome, in Alessandro Oradini's spacious apartment on the Via della Conciliazione, two stunned cardinals—quite old and indeed nervous—took measure of their situation.

"If Pietro's death sparks an investigation into his financial empire, it could do us severe damage, Andrea."

Andrea Vannucci nodded. "We must make sure there are no documents that could tie us to Montaldo's finances."

"We were wise to support his needs in cash. But we can't be certain that we won't be linked to him. Some fool always leaves some kind of paper trail in matters like this. Appointment books, notebooks, journals," Oradini said ruefully.

"But, Alessandro, there might not be an investigation. Pietro could have died naturally."

Don't be so naive, old friend, Oradini thought as he walked to the window of his apartment and looked down onto the Via della Conciliazione. Leaning a bit forward—his forehead almost touching the tall pane of glass—he could see the piazza where it was thought Saint Peter himself was crucified. "That's wishful thinking, Andrea. That's wishful thinking."

Aidan Kempe squeezed into the back seat of a taxi with Tom Fenton and Herm Volker.

"Fiumicino Airport," Kempe barked at the driver.

151

What was supposed to have been a long celebratory weekend in Rome honoring their leader's red hat had turned suddenly into a confusing nightmare. The news that Montaldo had been found dead in his hotel room changed everything.

Volker, looking straight ahead, said, "He looked fine at the banquet. Maybe a little tired, but overall he seemed to enjoy the attention, the tributes."

"Did he have any health issues that you knew of, Aidan?" Fenton asked.

"None that I was aware of. But that's not the kind of thing he would have confided in me. Our mysterious leader, known only as 'M' to most of the Brotherhood, remained pretty much a mysterious figure even to me. I met with him personally only a half-dozen times. Most of our communication was by fax, some phone calls."

The three Baltimore priests rode in anxious silence.

Aidan Kempe looked out the window of the cab without being able to focus his attention where he wanted it. For some reason, he couldn't stop thinking of Giorgio Grotti.

37

Cardinal Charles Cullen and Bishop Bryn Martin sat across from his Eminence, Cardinal Andrew Stockton, an Irish-born veteran of the church's diplomatic corps who had been chosen three years previously, to the surprise of most of the Vatican's establishment, to head the powerful Congregation for Bishops.

"I'd like to thank you, Your Eminence, for seeing us on such short notice."

Stockton nodded. "Like yourselves, I'm sure, we in the curia are stunned by the death of Cardinal Montaldo. May God give him eternal rest and peace."

"Bishop Martin and I thought we should take this opportunity to brief you personally on what we have come to know about a secret society—or perhaps a number of secret societies—that may have been connected to Cardinal Montaldo." Cullen lowered his voice. "We are keenly aware that Cardinal Montaldo has yet to be mourned and that his funeral is still to be planned, but we feel compelled to speak to you about our concerns before returning to the States."

Stockton shifted somewhat uncomfortably in his leather chair as Cullen continued.

"You remember, I'm sure, that my predecessor, Archbishop Wilfred Gunnison, died tragically in the midst of the celebration of his golden jubilee as a priest. His death was pronounced a suicide, an apparent reaction to public allegations of his sexual abuse of minors. Bishop Martin and I believe the archbishop was a member of one of these societies that included a handful of priests from the Archdiocese of Baltimore among their members. My own chancellor and financial secretary at the time, and not Archbishop Gunnison, was the leader of this group, who called themselves the Brotherhood of the Sacred Purple."

Cullen glanced at Martin as if for support.

"I was Cardinal Cullen's auxiliary bishop at the time, your Eminence," Martin said. "We discovered that the Brotherhood had defrauded the archdiocese of hundreds of thousands of dollars to further their mission to return the church to its pre-Vatican II state and to promote the ecclesiastical careers of priests and bishops who thought as they did. We also determined that the Brotherhood was being directed by a Vatican bishop: Pietro Montaldo."

Martin tried to read Cardinal Stockton's reaction, but the cardinal's face remained expressionless.

"After coming to Cleveland, I encountered a small but similar secret society that referred to itself as the Sentinels of the Supreme Center. This society shared the same mission as the Brotherhood of the Sacred Purple. I am convinced it planned and executed the murder of two women in my diocese who were ordained priests by a rogue bishop."

"It's important, Bishop," Stockton broke in, "to emphasize that those women only *attempted* ordination to the priesthood."

Martin accepted the correction without comment.

Cullen cleared his throat. "Cardinal Montaldo's driver, Eminence, a man by the name of Giorgio Grotti, was in Baltimore at the time of Archbishop Gunnison's death and in Cleveland when an attempt was made on Bishop Martin's own life."

Stockton showed no reaction to Cullen's revelation.

"It's clear to us that this Giorgio Grotti was more than Cardinal Montaldo's driver. He was an agent, an 'operative' if you will, of Cardinal Montaldo. He was his paid assassin. We are convinced that Archbishop Gunnison didn't commit suicide. We think he was murdered by Grotti."

"It should be no small consolation to you both," Stockton said, "that this congregation regularly receives reports of so called 'secret societies' of bishops, priests, and laity who might be called 'traditionalists.' They come from various countries. Spain, Germany, and now from the United States. They have never once proven to be of any substance. We receive similar reports, as you must know, of secret societies who strive to influence the church with very liberal and progressive objectives that are in no way in harmony with the magisterium.

"The only factual allegation you have made is that you have evidence of fraud or embezzlement on the part of your former financial secretary in Baltimore," Stockton said. "You can, of course, Cardinal Cullen, press civil charges against him or ask the Vatican's prosecutors to investigate the matter. You understand that should you choose the latter path, your oversight of the patrimony of the archdiocese would be subject to extensive review. Furthermore, what you and Bishop Martin *believe* about Cardinal Montaldo and his so-called secret societies might be true, but it remains your *belief*. And I can say the same about your allegations against the cardinal's driver, the man you *believe* to be an assassin."

Stockton held Cullen's gaze for a moment, then abruptly stood up. Cullen and Martin followed his lead. The meeting was over. An awkward silence followed the cardinal's summary and persisted through their curt dismissal from his esteemed presence. Standing at the door of his Vatican office as they were parting, Cardinal Stockton said with practiced formality, "May you each have a safe journey home. *Vade in pace.*"

38

So what are you going to do?" Vittoria Massi asked Grotti as they sat in the living room of her small apartment on Via dell'Umiltà.

"The medical examiner's report will be important. If it's death by natural causes, that gives me all the time I need. If they rule Montaldo's death a homicide, then I have to get out of Rome, and out of Italy, as soon as I can."

"You'll be okay, Giorgio. Trust me, the cause of death will be reported as a natural coronary failure. A high level of potassium in a body after death is completely unremarkable."

"I hope you're right," Grotti said warily.

"Here's another reason, more important than science, that it will be ruled a natural death. The Vatican will do everything it can to get the report that is best for its purposes. The last thing they want on their hands is the murder of a cardinal, especially right after his induction into the College of Cardinals."

Massi looked squarely at Grotti, pleased with her analysis. He stood suddenly and went to the window, peeking carefully out at the street below.

"You can't stay here. You understand that, don't you?"

"Of course I understand," Grotti said sharply. "I hope you're right about cause of death. That will give me some time. You see, I have a score to settle. Angelo betrayed me. I can't let that pass."

Massi thought for a moment. "Don't be so sure. I can't believe Angelo would do that."

"It had to be Angelo. It wasn't you. Who else could it have been?"

"I heard from one of Leonine's bodyguards that the don himself had a private meeting with Bishop Martin at Café Sant'Eustachio last Friday. It is more likely the don who tipped authorities that you had been assigned to assassinate the two Americans."

Grotti stood at the window thinking. "You know for certain that the don met with Martin?"

Massi frowned. "For certain."

It was enough for Grotti. Settling a score with Angelo was one thing. Striking out at the don of a Mafia family was another. He would be dead within twenty-four hours.

"Why would Scarano do such a thing?"

"He's a very…a very complicated man, Giorgio. He's not easy to read. I know he thought Montaldo was the worst of the corrupted bishops and cardinals inside the Vatican. And he took pains to meet with Bishop Martin the very day he arrived. You were betrayed, yes, but not by Angelo."

Grotti spun back from the window and sat down on Massi's couch, trying to process what he had just heard and discern what he should do next.

"I'll wait until the cause of death comes out. Then I'm out of here. Thanks to Montaldo, I have a Vatican passport and a Colombian passport in addition to my Italian one."

"Where will you go?"

"Better you don't know, Vittoria. Better for both of us."

39

Bishop Martin? Party of six?"

"That's us," Martin said to the hostess.

She led them to a rectangular table in the corner of Taverna Giulia where Cullen and Martin took the two end seats, with Nora and Ian on one side and Margaret and Ella on the other. Martin ordered two bottles of Sangiovese and the *Fantasia di Antipasti* as his guests picked up their menus.

"I've been here a few times," Ian said, "and the *Pansotti con Pesto di Noci* is really exquisite. Any of their pastas with pesto should be remarkable."

A few minutes later the wine arrived, menus were put aside, and the conversation was joined. Neither the cardinal nor the bishop felt inclined to mention the frosty reception they had endured in Stockton's high-ceilinged, elegant curial office.

"So," Cullen said, "I understand the four of you visited the Forum this afternoon."

"Ella and I had lunch at the Roof Garden restaurant. We were in the balcony, so to speak," said Margaret, "while Nora and Ian were walking the dusty streets of ancient Rome. This is my first visit, and probably my last. I'll be sorting it all out for months, I'm sure."

"We'll all be sorting this experience out for months," Ella said. "This must have been so difficult for you, Charles, and you, Bryn, knowing that you might be in serious danger. It had to color every moment."

Cullen moved his menu aside. "I'm glad the Carabinieri took the warning Bryn received at face value. Lorenzo Tosco and his Vatican police force have helped a great deal, too. I think Tosco has been doing all he can."

"Speaking of Tosco, he called me just before we left the hotel," Martin said. "They got the coroner's report on Montaldo's death. It will be released tomorrow by the Carabinieri, and the Vatican Press Office will follow with an official statement." Martin paused as every eye at the table rose to meet his. "Acute myocardial infarction."

"A natural death," said Cullen sourly. "I don't think we should be surprised. Not at all."

"What do you make of that, Bryn?" Nora asked.

"I'm thinking Giorgio Grotti is very good at his job."

Cullen cast a glance between them. "But maybe, just maybe, we were too quick to blame Grotti for Montaldo's death. We don't really know that. His employer was just made a cardinal, for God's sake! It's not up to us to figure out how Montaldo died. Let the Carabinieri deal with that."

"You're right, Charles," Martin said. "Our real concern is whether the threat Grotti posed has passed. I think it has. Sure, he may still be loose somewhere in Rome right now. But the notes must have come from him, and I firmly believe that he no longer aims to harm us. I probably wouldn't be sitting here if I believed otherwise. So, let me change topics. While the four of you were enjoying Rome this afternoon, Charles and I met with the prefect of the Congregation for Bishops, Cardinal Andrew Stockton."

Their waiter approached with the *antipasti* and proceeded to take orders for their main plates. Cullen waited impatiently for him to finish before he picked up on the story.

"It didn't go well, to tell you the truth. Cardinal Stockton didn't want to hear a thing we had to say. He dismissed our concerns about Montaldo's secret societies and his methods to save the church from heretics as mere conjecture."

Martin shook his head in dismay. "I had heard before how dismissively the curia treats diocesan bishops. But we personally felt its heavy hand fall down on us this afternoon. It was as steely an exercise of hierarchical control as I could ever imagine."

"It was as if Stockton was saying, 'I don't want to hear your nonsensical suspicions about a bishop who worked in a position of trust in the Vatican for years, this archbishop, this cardinal.' He completely ignored our assertion that Wilfred was murdered and that three murders in Cleveland were tied to Montaldo's societies." Cullen's face was reddening. "He was telling us to take our foolish suspicions and go home."

"One thing struck me as odd, though," Martin said. "As Stockton was showing us the door, he said, *"Vade in pace."*

"The very words in the notes from Giorgio Grotti," Cullen said.

Cullen was the first to notice Cardinal Andrew Stockton being seated at a table some thirty feet away. He was in the company of Cardinals Oradini and Vannucci and a young priest who looked to be in his thirties. They did not seem to have noticed Cullen and his group.

"Don't look now," Cullen said to Martin, whose back was to the new arrivals, "but Stockton has just been seated with a party of admirers. I've heard the Taverna Giulia is popular with the Vatican crowd. I guess I shouldn't be surprised."

Martin didn't turn, but Nora, Ian, Margaret, and Ella all glanced at the four dinner guests settling in.

Nora asked, "Do we know who the others are?"

Martin cheated a glance behind him. Cullen, Martin, and Ian caught one another's eyes, and each flashed a quick smile.

Cullen announced, "Cardinal Stockton is in the company of Cardinals Oradini and Vannucci. I don't know the priest. He's probably Stockton's secretary." Cullen again looked quickly at Martin and Ian, who knew pretty much what he was going to say next. "Cardinals Oradini and Vannucci were patrons of the late Pietro Montaldo. They...*facilitated* his career in the curia and his steady rise to bishop, archbishop, and finally cardinal. They are two prominent leaders of the antediluvian wing of the College of Cardinals. They are all so sure the Second Vatican Council was a huge mistake that did irreparable harm to the church."

Ella and Margaret caught a whiff of suspense. Both women enjoyed holding front-row seats to an ecclesial drama unimagined by people outside the clergy. "So this is how it actually works," Margaret whispered to Ella.

"Not only are they the leaders of the traditionalist wing of the curia," Ian added. "They are old warriors. For a generation and more they have used their personal wealth and the wealth of conservative laity, their networks, their media outlets, their bloggers, their secret societies—and whatever else it takes—to bring the church back to its pre-Vatican II state of law and order, it's once transcendent position of dignity and mystery."

Cullen finally caught Stockton's eye. The two cardinals exchanged a thin smile of recognition and returned to their table talk.

Stockton signaled brusquely to the nearest waiter. "I'd like to send a bottle of champagne with my compliments to the table of six in the corner. One that's not too dear, please. A Chandon Brut perhaps."

Dismissing the waiter, he turned back to his guests and continued a summary of his adept handling of Cullen and Martin earlier in the day. Oradini and Vannucci appeared only mildly interested in Stockton's account. Each man was no doubt calculating the weight of scandal that would befall him if Cullen and

Martin's allegations ever reached the secular media.

The young priest accompanying them hung on every word, like a first-year graduate student listening to his dissertation director. This Monday-evening dinner at the Taverna Giulia, the up-and-coming young man understood quite correctly, had become a real-life seminar on how thorny issues are settled, buried, or ignored at the Vatican. More importantly, it was an invaluable lesson on how to scramble to the top of the ecclesial ladder.

A few minutes later, Cardinal Cullen watched with interest as a waiter arrived with a silver cart, atop of which sat a bottle of champagne, six flutes, and an ice bucket. "Congratulations, Cardinal Cullen! The champagne is compliments of Cardinal Stockton."

Cullen nodded thanks to Stockton, who in turn nodded back.

Ella Landers turned to Margaret and said softly, "This little scene takes me back to my days in the Foreign Service. I always thought of it as 'civil treachery.'"

They sat in silence while the waiter poured champagne into their bubbling flutes with an adept flourish, then raised their glasses to toast his Eminence, Cardinal Charles Cullen.

"Where were we before this...kind gesture from Cardinal Stockton?" Cullen asked.

"We were linking his dinner companions to efforts by Cardinal Montaldo to have you both popped," Ian said haughtily, lifting the bottle from the bucket by its neck and inspecting its label with a frown. "So, Stockton himself appears to be a significant player in the movement back to the real, true, and static church. That helps explain Montaldo's move to Perugia as archbishop."

"And sheds a bright light on how Montaldo was named a cardinal," Nora added.

"That's the question I have been asking all along," Margaret said.

The *antipasti* plates and tray were cleared as waiters approached the table with their entrées.

"Let's pivot from the dark side for the moment and enjoy this food while it's hot," Martin proposed.

After Cullen led the table in grace, the conversation shifted to practical matters. How early would the hotel restaurant be open for breakfast? When would their coaches be ready for boarding? Martin passed the Sangiovese down the table and savored the first bite of his entrée.

As the waitstaff cleared their plates a while later, Martin said to Margaret, "Before I get to my main point about how a man like Montaldo can rise in an organization of the faithful, let me bring you and Ella up to date. You know I met on Friday night with Leonine Scarano, the mob boss who warned us. What you don't know is that he explained in some detail how Montaldo's networks are financed."

Martin paused and snuck a glance over his shoulder at Stockton's table. They looked like they were getting ready to leave.

"The don told me that it was widely known in Rome's banking world and in some corners of the Vatican that the fathers of Cardinals Oradini and Vannucci, both in the banking business, made fortunes at the end of World War II by assisting the Vatican's start up bank, the Institute for Religious Works, to help Nazi leaders find safe havens in South America. The accumulated wealth of the fathers was passed on to their sons."

Martin took a sip of wine. He decided not to mention the rumors that the cardinals' fathers were Nazi spies during the war, working for years with Vatican insiders.

"Scarano also told me that Montaldo headed up an unofficial institute he called the 'Pontifical Purse for the Poor.' Apparently it was a favorite charity for wealthy conservative Catholics. I mention all this because the late Cardinal Montaldo had very substantial financial strength for his crusade to save the church from its enemies."

Cullen watched as Stockton and his party rose and left without a glance in their direction.

Ella smiled. "Having unlimited funds and friends in high places has never hurt anyone's career. You certainly have whetted our appetites, Bryn. Don't keep us in suspense. What's your point?"

"Pietro Montaldo mastered the art of what I'm calling 'whitemail,' which is almost the opposite of blackmail. Keep in mind this is personal conjecture. But I think it's a plausible explanation of how Montaldo made it to the Red Hat Club. Here's what I'm getting at. Montaldo gathered as much personal information as he could on his Vatican colleagues, especially negative personal information. He found out how they were milking the Vatican's finances. Until very recently, that was pretty easy to do. A lot of cardinals and bishops lead pretty lush lives. Expensive furnishings for their well-appointed apartments, pricey art collections, elaborate entertaining, that sort of thing. Far too much spending to be covered by their relatively modest salaries. Montaldo learned where their money came from. And often these sources of income would be embarrassing to the prelate if they came to light. And then, of course, there's sex. While most of the Vatican clerics, high and low, lead celibate lives or at least struggle to do so, a sizeable minority are sexually active. I'm surmising from my conversation with the don that Montaldo knew of clerics and prelates who visited the prostitutes around the Roma Termini, one of the major areas of prostitution in Rome. Prostitution is legal in Italy, by the way. But brothels aren't. It's not hard to imagine that his spies also made him aware of prelates involved in secret love affairs with members of either sex. What I'm saying is that I think Montaldo *had something* on many movers and shakers in the Vatican."

Nora leaned in toward her brother. "There is an interesting psychological aspect to all this, Bryn. From that perspective, Montaldo exercised a great deal of latent power. You had to tiptoe around him, making sure that staying in his good graces was always front of mind. If you worked in the Vatican, you did not want to get on his bad side."

"Charles and I managed to do just that from across the Atlantic. But let me stay with Margaret's original question about the rise to power. Montaldo, armed as he is with this knowledge, doesn't blackmail his colleagues. He does exactly the opposite. He 'whitemails' them. Instead of extorting money, he gives them money. He gives them gifts on their birthdays, on their ordination anniversaries, for their 'special apostolic projects.' Now these colleagues suspect or know outright that Montaldo has the goods on them. But he doesn't ask to be bought off. He does the *opposite* and gives them money. He protects their secrets and at the same time is very generous. If my theory is right, very few at the Vatican would ever have spoken ill of him. And many will have spoken highly of him in private."

"Whew!" Margaret wheezed. "It makes sense to me."

"What you're describing," said Ian, "has been the *modus operandi* for wealthy church careerists for centuries, especially in the fifteen and sixteenth centuries. But you've just coined the perfect phrase—'whitemail.' I love it! Machiavelli would give Montaldo high marks."

Yes, Martin thought, *Machiavelli would approve of Montaldo's use of power. Maybe he would have learned a lesson or two himself.* He looked at his watch. "Let's continue this conversation on the flight home. Right now, I'd like to get back to the hotel. We have a long day ahead of us tomorrow."

No one in Martin's dinner party noticed a solitary figure seated at the bar of the Taverna Giulia. Paolo Corsi, the gendarme assigned to shadow the American prelates, took out his cell phone and held down a button.

"Don Scarano? It's Corsi. They're just leaving the restaurant. I'll follow them to the hotel."

"Good. We will take care of the rest."

40

Giorgio Grotti, driving his dark green Ferrari 488 GTB, slipped into the traffic heading north on A1, Strada Statale. He was smirking. Without Montaldo nagging him to slow down, he would make the 175-kilometer drive to Perugia in ninety minutes easily. He moved smoothly into the high-speed lane, feeling a sudden rush of freedom. Vittoria had been right. The coroner ruled that Montaldo had a heart attack.

Grotti enjoyed the power of the Ferrari's 3.9-liter twin-turbocharged engine and let its low roar charge his own swelling psychic energy. A certain lightness of being seemed to settle over him. The sky was overcast, but the clouds were high and thin. The sun would break through before long. He had been living, he now understood, a life in the shadows. But no longer. He was free of the dark rooms in the basement of Montaldo's episcopal palace. He was no longer a chauffeur. He was calling the shots now. Had his execution of Montaldo's orders made him a mere mercenary? An assassin for hire? So be it. Was he still a soldier doing what was necessary in defense of the true faith? Grotti winced at his prior naiveté. No more. Not since discovering the wretched perversions of his former employer. Montaldo liked to have sex with men. Why had Giorgio never suspected this? Worse, the cardinal preferred sex with young male prostitutes, almost boys. It had taken a while for Angelo's portrait of Montaldo to sink in. But when it did, it changed everything. All these years Grotti had thought of himself as a warrior on secret, sacred missions. But he had really been no more than an executioner for a pervert. Montaldo had never come on to him, though from time to time he had caught the archbishop's admiring glances at his muscled frame. Hurtling down the Strada Statale, a light seemed to flash on. *So that explains Dunmore's and Ashley's privileged status in the archbishop's palace.*

A grim smile crossed Grotti's face. Why shouldn't he still enjoy his dispensation to kill for the good of the church? Why should Montaldo's sudden death cancel the dispensation? And for the first time since dispatching Montaldo, the irony struck him. He thought of Montaldo's last moments, the look of disbelief, the sudden fear, when Grotti pressed the chloroform-soaked cloth to his face.

"What are you doing?" were the last garbled words to escape the condemned man's mouth.

In hindsight, Grotti realized what he should have said to the terrified cardinal cowering in his grasp. "It's all right, *Eminenza*, I have been granted a special dispensation to kill."

41

Father Trace Dunmore looked at the clock on the mantel above the dying embers in the fireplace of his living room. It was 11:30 at night. The household staff had either gone home or were asleep in their beds. Montaldo's episcopal palace was silent, locked down for the night. Armed with a flashlight and wearing medical exam gloves, he slipped out of his suite and climbed the carpeted stairs to the third floor. Dunmore paused at the top and listened for any sound of movement. All was quiet. Hoping the floorboards under the carpet runner wouldn't squeak, he moved down the wide hall, past walls graced by the works of Perugian masters, to the double doors of Montaldo's spacious suite.

Dunmore reached for the handle, glanced to his right and left, and entered the dark living room. With his flashlight beam on the floor ahead of him, he walked softly, cautiously, toward the French doors of Montaldo's study. Once inside he moved to the small adjacent room the archbishop used as his workspace. That's where the documents, ledgers, records, and other incriminating papers Dunmore was seeking would be stored. The room was rectangular, twenty feet by ten feet he guessed. A thin curtain covered a tall single window guarded by heavy dark green velvet drapes, only partially drawn. The desk in the middle of the room was half the size of the ornate monster in the study. The desktop appeared to be orderly—a stack of folders with a paper weight keeping them in place, a cordless phone, a personal computer, a letter opener, a pen. A fax machine stood on a small table off to one side. Dunmore went straight to the four-drawer cabinet against the wall to his left. One drawer held files of memos, directives, and correspondence dealing with Montaldo's work as Director of the Office of Pontifical Protocol before he was named Archbishop of Perugia. Dunmore smiled. Montaldo certainly was careful. The labels attached to the folders in the other drawers read: Fraternities, Sodalities, Oratories, Retreats, Associates. What he was looking for—records, notes, or correspondence dealing with the Sentinels of the Supreme Center and the Brotherhood of the Sacred Purple—must lie buried somewhere in these innocently labeled folders, folders he flipped through but didn't have time to properly scrutinize.

A framed photograph placed on a bookshelf caught his eye. It was a photo of men in military dress, Montaldo among them, seated in a Jeep with two army comrades. On the back of another group photo a label read "Intelligence Unit" with five names listed below. The second name was Captain Pietro Montaldo, unit leader. The archbishop had never mentioned his military background. Strangely, there were no photos of Montaldo's parents, or of any siblings. No family photos at all. Before returning to the study, Dunmore's torch beam caught an elegantly framed painting of St. Aloysius Gonzaga. *Family of a sort, I guess.*

Dunmore quietly closed the door to Montaldo's workspace and walked in semidarkness to a chair in front of the cardinal's desk. He sat down, thinking of the countless meetings he and Simon had endured with the cardinal, seated in these very chairs. All of that now over in a flash. Montaldo's high-backed leather chair was turned facing the fireplace against the back wall of the study. Dunmore sat for a moment in the darkened study trying to slow his racing heart, straining to figure out what to do after the surreal events of the last two days. The Papal Mass, the triumphal banquet, the shocking death of a new cardinal.

The shocking *murder* of his benefactor. Should he return to England, to his mother's stuffy circle of clipped aristocratic friends? Should he stay in Perugia and await the naming of the new archbishop? Maybe a man who would keep him on as his master of ceremonies. Montaldo's death was now safely on record as due to natural causes. *Nothing to fear,* he told himself, *with the Carabinieri.* He would never be implicated in the murder of His Eminence, Pietro Montaldo.

As the priest moved to stand, Montaldo's desk chair creaked and slowly began to turn. Dunmore raised a fist to his mouth to stifle a rising scream.

Giorgio Grotti said softly, "Good evening, Father Dunmore."

"What the hell are you doing here?"

"I've been waiting for you, Father."

Dunmore was trembling now, his eyes wide, his mouth gaping open.

"Put your flashlight down," Grotti ordered as he turned his own flashlight beam onto Dunmore's startled face. The priest's pupils, to Grotti, looked like raisins, dark and shrunken and small. "You won't find anything incriminating in there, Father. I've already looked. But you and your friend Simon Ashley might one day incriminate me."

"No, we'd never do that! We didn't tell the police anything. You know that!"

"Ah, that's true, Father. But you might someday be tempted to relate to the authorities my late-night visit to the new cardinal's suite the night he passed on."

"No! Ashley and I would never do that."

"Sorry, Father, but I know only one way to be sure."

42

Bryn Martin had his phone set on vibrate in the boarding area of Fiumicino Airport when he felt it stir in his breast pocket. He stepped away to answer it.

"Hello."

"Bishop Martin?"

"Yes, this is Bishop Martin."

"This is Lorenzo Tosco. Do you have a moment?"

"I do. I'm at the gate waiting for our flight back to the States, but we're not boarding just yet."

"I'm afraid I have some disturbing news. Early this morning, in Cardinal Montaldo's episcopal palace, Father Trace Dunmore, the cardinal's master of ceremonies, was found dead at the foot of a long staircase. His neck was broken, apparently in a fall. Perugian authorities are investigating. I thought you should know. Do I remember correctly that Father Dunmore worked for you in Cleveland?"

"Yes, he was chancellor of the diocese for a short time when I first arrived."

"My condolences, Bishop Martin."

Martin remained silent. Finally, he said, "Thank you, Inspector. Do you know the whereabouts of Simon Ashley? He was a friend of Father Dunmore and taught for a short time at a university in Cleveland."

"I know who he is, but we here in Rome know nothing of his whereabouts. Perhaps the Perugian Carabinieri would know."

"He might be in danger. I'm not sure Father Dunmore's death was an accident."

"I understand, Bishop. We'll try to locate him. He checked out of the Cavalieri Hotel with Father Dunmore early yesterday." Tosco waited for Martin to say something, but the bishop was again silent. "On another note, Bishop, you might want to know that the Gendarmerie and the Carabinieri were not the only ones looking out for you and Cardinal Cullen."

"What do you mean?"

"It seems that Leonine Scarano has had one or more of his bodyguards keeping an eye on you and the cardinal since you arrived in Rome."

"He said something the night we talked about me never being quite so safe, despite the threat, as when I was with him last Friday at the coffee house."

"My men. His men."

Martin smiled. "How blessed were we? The angels of light and the angels of darkness too, all watching over us."

Martin walked back over to Cullen, who was seated with Ian, Nora, Ella, and Margaret. He motioned to them to follow him over to the window overlooking the tarmac. Their Boeing 777 was being prepped for its impending transatlantic flight. Martin watched as the slow-moving escalator trundled luggage and bundles of various sizes into the fat belly of the plane. A food catering truck rose on its hydraulic jack toward an open door close to the front of the plane.

"I just had a call from Tosco," Martin said in a whisper.

His five friends leaned in a little closer, creating a tight circle around him.

"Trace Dunmore was found dead a few hours ago in Montaldo's episcopal palace. His neck was broken. The story they're telling is that he fell down a long staircase and suffered a fatal injury."

No one spoke at first. Martin looked at Cullen, who simply shook his head in disbelief.

"Holy Mother of God!" Cullen said to no one in particular. "Is this never going to end? This has got to be the work of Grotti."

An announcement brought them back to the moment. "May I have your attention, please," a United Airlines agent said, speaking into a portable microphone at the doorway of their gate. "Passengers in premium class and others needing special assistance are now welcome to board Flight 72 to Newark, New Jersey."

Martin, Cullen, and the others returned to their seats to pick up their carry-on bags. Martin smiled at the Merrimans and the others in Cullen's official party who caught his eye. He envied them their ignorance of the tragic drama surrounding the elevation of Charles Cullen to the College of Cardinals. For them, it had been a weekend never to be forgotten: the consistory, the reception in the Aula Paulus VI, the Papal Mass, and the dinner at La Compana. And it was a weekend to remember for Charles Cullen and Bryn Martin and their inner circle as well—but for very different reasons.

Boarding took forty-five minutes. Cullen's main party enjoyed premium class seating for the flight home. Cullen, Martin, Nora, and Ian were shoulder to shoulder in bulkhead seats. Margaret and Ella were just across the aisle.

Martin, though exhausted from the high drama of their long weekend, doubted he would sleep at all during the nine-hour flight. More than sleep, he needed to sort things out with Nora. His sister's spiritual perspective and psychological training, without fail, had shed a fresh light on almost every crisis he ever faced. Nora was the most centered and balanced person he knew. Her mix of insight, wisdom, and perspective had always lifted him up at just the right moment.

"You look tired, Bryn," Nora said as they fastened their seat belts.

"A good night's sleep would be a godsend. But more than that, I'm in dire need of a consult with an exceptionally insightful psychologist. And, dear sister, I'm expecting my normal family discount."

Nora smiled genuinely for the first time in days. "You'll pay, big brother, one way or another."

With that, the plane shifted and started its slow but steady backward move away from the gate, away, at last, from Rome.

43

Thirty-four thousand feet above the Atlantic

The meal was served and cleared, and the flight attendants soon began pushing drink carts through the cabin. Cullen and Martin sipped black coffee. Nora and Ian had asked for herbal tea.

"What do you make of Leonine Scarano's role in all of this?" Cullen asked Martin.

"He's no Robin Hood. I doubt if even a sliver of his illegal wealth reaches the poor. But I don't know. There seems to be a ray of grace in the man. Look at his behavior, Charles. Before we even leave for Rome, he gets word to us that we need to be careful, that we'll be in danger. Then he invites me to a meeting that lasts for almost an hour, telling me more about Montaldo and his secret societies in sixty minutes than I learned in all the years with you in Baltimore, in all my dealings with the Sentinels of the Supreme Center in Cleveland. Then we learn he was looking out for us the whole time.

"In our brief meeting in the bar, I sensed two things about him—his intelligence and his passion," Cullen said thoughtfully.

"He made a good match for Giorgio Grotti, that's for sure," Martin replied.

"It was good of you to introduce us during dinner at La Compana."

"I thought he deserved to meet you, and you deserved to meet him."

"When I get home, Bryn, I'm going to fly him some Baltimore crab cakes."

The cardinal and the bishop fell silent, surprised and grateful for the help that came their way unbidden, from unpredictable places.

Nora turned slightly to her left a short while later and was pleased to see her brother at last dozing peacefully.

Forty minutes later, now high over the Atlantic, Martin opened his eyes. Cullen was reading. Nora and Ian were trying to sleep. But he felt as if his batteries had been fully recharged.

"Do you mind if we talk for a bit?" he asked his sister as he gently elbowed her.

"Okay, but let me get some more tea."

Ian was fully awake by the time she returned.

"Let's talk about Giorgio Grotti," Bryn said to Nora.

"Well, as you can imagine, I've been thinking of Grotti for some time now. But let me tell you first of a client I had a number of years ago. Let's just call him…George."

Cullen put his book down and Ian stirred and turned in interest.

"George was from a devout Catholic family. He grew up in the 1950s when there was still a heavy moralistic climate in the church. He began by telling me how angry he was with the Catholic Church." Nora turned to Ian. "You'll understand this, Ian. George was mad because he felt the church robbed him of any kind of joy or peace during his adolescent years. And it was primarily over sex. He bought hook, line, and sinker all the negativity the church preached about sex, that any sexual thought, desire, or action outside of marriage was a mortal sin. It came down to this: He was plagued by guilt about his sexual curiosity and urges. He felt guilty about being a normal teenage boy."

Nora sipped her fresh cup of tea. "He thought maybe he should be a priest. You know, just put the whole sex thing on a shelf. Be celibate. Be a hero to his mother. Be somebody special. Of course, that didn't happen. It took a long time and a lot of hard work for George to get free of the deep connection the church had forged in him between sex and shame."

"Did he ever get his head completely above water?" Cullen asked.

"He did, Charles. As far as I know, he's doing pretty well. He felt a deep despair over issues with the church that would from time to time explode into rage, or it's dark sister, depression. Last I heard, he was married and had a couple young kids. But here's why I told you a little about George. George and Giorgio are not that different."

Cullen was by now leaning over Martin's seat to catch Nora's analysis. Both Margaret and Ella were leaning to listen in. Ian moved his seatback into a reclined position to accommodate them.

Nora looked to Martin and Cullen, then turned to the others. They reminded her of graduate students in a doctoral seminar. "George carried a resentment embedded deep in his psyche, or soul, if you prefer. A resentment directed at the church, a church he had been raised to love. So he tried to smother his resentment. Not give it air to breathe. It took him years to understand why he was so depressed, why he could lose it from time to time." Nora paused. "Are you with me?"

Martin spoke for them all. "I think so. Go on."

"It's likely that Giorgio Grotti, like my client George, has carried an onus of resentment and simmering anger around with him since he was a teenager. But Giorgio's suppressed anger isn't connected with Catholic guilt in the same way George's was. But like George, his anger is connected with sex."

"Most Italian men," Ian offered, "aren't particularly troubled in conscience when it comes to sex. Fidelity and chastity are viewed more as ideals, things that a man might strive for, but…"

"Here's why I think Giorgio Grotti's anger is so linked to sex," Nora resumed. Then she abruptly paused—an unnaturally long pause. "I suspect Grotti is homosexual himself."

Her air-born seminar members fell silent, as if the oxygen had been sucked from the cabin. Seconds passed before anyone could respond.

"Tell us why you think that," Ella said.

"Giorgio Grotti was raised a Catholic…and we know the church teaches that a homosexual orientation is itself an intrinsically disordered condition. But Giorgio's battle, if I'm correct here, isn't just about the church but with masculine Italian culture as well. The teenage Giorgio Grotti didn't want to be gay. So he tells himself he is not gay. He represses his same-sex desires. He denies them. He tells himself that he is straight. He is 'normal.' He flirts with girls. He may even have intimate encounters with a few. But don't forget," Nora looked to Martin for confirmation, "he's devout enough in his Catholicism to enter the seminary."

"Yes," Bryn said decisively. "I heard from Scarano…or maybe it was Tosco…both of them, I think, told me Grotti was expelled for attacking a seminarian who came on to him. He put him in the hospital."

"That kind of overreactive response sounds like rage to me," Nora said. "And it would fit the picture of Grotti that I think is likely. So he joins the Carabinieri. It's like a gay American man in denial joining the Marines to affirm his masculinity."

"And then," Martin adds, "somehow, someway, he goes to work for Montaldo and becomes his 'special ops' man, his assassin in the war to save the church. But then he learns sometime

179

before this consistory, with the plan for our assassinations already rolling, that Montaldo is gay. And probably that Montaldo likes young men, almost boys. Scarano said as much when we had our coffee-house meeting. Those guys would not have withheld that part of Montaldo's behavior from Grotti."

"That fits with what Tom Hathaway told me when we met at the Angelicum," Ian said. "Montaldo had a reputation within the Vatican and at the pontifical seminaries for hitting on young, attractive students."

"So," Nora resumed, "it at last dawns on Grotti that he hates pederasts more than he hates heretics."

"And he realizes that the real heretic in his war on behalf of Montaldo was Montaldo himself." The irony hit Martin. "And the cardinal's assassin assassinates the cardinal."

44

Having made it through customs at the Newark airport, Cardinal Charles Cullen and Bishop Bryn Martin stood together near the bar in the United Club, where they had gone to kill a few hours between flights. Both men were aching to sleep in their own beds.

"Excuse me a moment, Bryn," Cullen said, "I want to chat a bit with my 'official' party before they scatter." Cullen colored slightly as he moved toward the chancery crowd and lay leaders who had accompanied them on the trip to the consistory.

Martin's phone vibrated. "Hello."

"Bishop Martin?"

"Yes."

"This is Lorenzo Tosco again. I hoped I might catch you on the ground."

"We just landed. We've got a little wait for our connecting flights."

Tosco paused. "I regret to tell you that the sacristan of San Lorenzo, Perugia's cathedral, upon opening its doors for the morning's tourists, found Simon Ashley's body stuffed under a back pew. He had been strangled."

Martin felt a rising spasm of nausea. Montaldo, Dunmore, and now Ashley.

"Grotti?"

"It would appear so," Tosco said. "Everybody's looking for him—Europol, the Polizia di Stato, the Carabinieri. They'll get him, but it won't be easy. He's pretty smooth."

He's more than smooth, Martin thought. "Any developments on Father Dunmore's death?"

"We've heard nothing from the coroner's office. With Montaldo, Dunmore, and now Ashley dead within forty-eight hours of one another, I suspect they will be moving very quickly."

"Thanks for keeping us informed. And again, my thanks to you and your associates for looking after us. You were all terrific."

"You're very welcome, Bishop. Your meeting with Leonine Scarano was a real eye-opener for all of us. The fact that you didn't hesitate to meet with him wasn't lost on me. Nor, I suspect, on him."

Bryn Martin took a seat on the closest bar stool. Three deaths…three murders…all within two days. And Giorgio Gotti on the run. But that was only an assumption, Martin realized. Maybe he's hiding out somewhere in the shadows of the Vatican. Or plodding around the streets of Rome dressed as a nun.

This call about Ashley's death shook him deeply. *Is Grotti settling old scores? Or eliminating anyone who could possibly incriminate him in Montaldo's murder? Is he calculating…or is he crazy? And what other names might remain on his list?*

Politely waving a bartender away, Martin scanned the club's patrons looking for Nora. He had to update her before they boarded their separate connecting flights. He finally caught her eye and beckoned to her.

"Are you all right, Bryn?" she asked. "You look a little shaky."

"I'll confess I feel a little lightheaded right now. I just got some terrible news from Lorenzo Tosco. Simon Ashley, Montaldo's curator, was found strangled in the cathedral in Perugia. You met him in Cleveland last year."

"I remember him well. He was a classmate of Ian's."

"I'm sure Ashley was complicit in arranging the murders of Laura Spivak and Frances Hellerman."

"The women priests."

"And Dunmore was involved too. As far as I know they were the only Sentinels of the Supreme Center in Cleveland."

"Is everything okay?" the ever-observant Charles Cullen asked, approaching Bryn and Nora.

"Tosco just called," Bryn said, trying to look anywhere but into his friend's eyes. He shook his head as if to say, *You won't believe this.* "Simon Ashley was found strangled and stuffed under a pew in the Perugia cathedral."

Cullen took an unconscious look around before asking, "Grotti?"

"Looks that way. Tosco said everybody is looking for him— the Italian police, Europol."

Cullen waved to the bartender. "I think we could all use a drink."

Martin settled deeply into a comfortable United Club chair. Cullen sat next to him. Both were nursing ruby glasses of cabernet sauvignon.

"Here's my fear, Charles. What if Grotti has really gone over the edge? What if he now sees everyone who was associated with Montaldo—members of his secret societies, his Vatican cronies, his networks of orthodoxy police—as hopelessly corrupt, and plans to eliminate them one by one."

"I hadn't thought of that…that possibility," Cullen stammered, almost in a whisper.

"Scarano said Montaldo had special patrons, two cardinals—Alessandro Oradini and Andrea Vannucci."

"They were with him at the reception after the consistory."

"Do you think they could be in danger too?"

Cullen thought for a moment, and shrugged. "And then there is Aidan Kempe. He, Tom Fenton, and Herm Volker were all at the consistory as well. And Grotti knows Kempe."

Martin stood and stretched and pulled out his cell. "I guess I'd better call Inspector Tosco back."

45

Lausanne, Switzerland

Giorgio Grotti sat at an outdoor café that offered a perfect postcard view of Lake Geneva. The fresh mountain air and the transcendent beauty of the lake's smooth surface cuddled safely in the embrace of the Alps gave him a sense of what? Renewal? Relief? Then he realized it was the uplifting feeling he used to have stepping out of the confessional as a young boy: All was right; all was pure. Giorgio Grotti felt reborn.

The former chauffeur was wearing sunglasses, a white silk shirt with two buttons open at the neck, and a midnight blue suit, not looking at all the part of a tourist. He picked at a plate of fruit, black olives, and cheese. He knew he had to be careful right now. By this time, Europol might well be looking for him. But he had plenty of cash and would soon have more than he would ever need. He smiled, pleased with his 'Vade in pace' notes to the two bishops. *Nice touch*, he told himself. Yes, he had money...and his training as a Carabinieri Special Intervention Group operative would help keep him below the radar. At least for the time being, the odds appeared to be in his favor.

He would spend the night here in Lausanne, a bit safer, he thought, than staying a night in Geneva.

He ordered another glass of the house white wine...surprisingly good, as he had heard it would be. Grotti looked around.

Nothing suspicious. He had no desire to taste the night life of Lausanne or Geneva. It was too risky anyway. He'd pay cash for a light supper at this quaint café and get a good night's sleep. Over the years he had made regular trips to Credit Suisse for his boss. There would be no questions tomorrow when he made a final substantial withdrawal, closing Montaldo's various numbered accounts. A few more days here at Lausanne, staying at a different hotel each night, and he would be off to Canada. From there it would be easy enough to slip into the U.S. to take care of one final pressing matter.

The low sun of late afternoon softened the assassin's mood and threw long shadows across the lake. This is what he had been missing during his years with Montaldo. Nearness to nature. Cool, fresh breezes. *The easy flow of a simple life well lived.* Grotti caught himself. *The easy flow of a lavish life to be well lived.*

Grotti sipped his wine, contemplating the conversion he was experiencing. He stumbled at the term "conversion"—so rich in religious overtones. No, *his* conversion was not from sin to virtue or from nonbelief to faith. It was from smug certitude to reasonable doubt, from hypocrisy to reality, from the clarity of a good lie to the confounding conundrum of the truth. How had he missed the sordid underbelly of Montaldo's hyper-orthodoxy for so long? How had he harbored such self-righteous certitude about what was true and what was false about the faith? Maybe he had been willfully blind to it.

Grotti had met the Perugian bishop at the very apex of his own personal confusion, a moment of questioning everything. When he had fallen into despair, Montaldo had given him a sense of purpose in his life. More than that, the bishop had endowed him with a false feeling of heroism: *Work for me, and you will be a sacred warrior defending Christ's church from its enemies, without and within.* That's basically what the cardinal had said. *Work for me, and you will be a slayer of heretics who threaten the very life blood of the church.* And it hadn't hurt that he'd been paid handsomely. If Montaldo had seduced him, well, maybe he had wanted to be seduced.

In hindsight, Grotti could see that Montaldo played him with devilish cunning, knowing the words Grotti wanted so much to hear. *You are different,* Montaldo had said. *You are God's own avenging angel.*

Grotti remembered the scene as if it were yesterday. A successor of the apostles speaking to him with the authority of God, with sympathy, perhaps even with a bit of affection. *You were a seminarian, called by God,* the bishop had said, *a faithful Catholic, wrongly expelled for resisting a sexual advance. Come work with me to save the church from its enemies.* He remembered Montaldo pausing for effect. *There will be suffering, Giorgio. You will bear a cross.* Another pause. *No one else will truly understand what God is asking you to do. No one. You must be willing to live with that, Giorgio.* With those lofty sentiments, Grotti's seduction had been consummated. He had become an assassin.

Well, Cardinal Montaldo, wherever you are, I'm no longer willing to live with that. I'm still a lost soul, but I'm no longer willing to kill for you in the name of God. Grotti smiled. *But I am willing to kill to protect myself from the likes of you, Eminenza. And I'm afraid there is still one man who can implicate me—that priest in Baltimore, Monsignor Aidan Kempe.*

46

Baltimore, Maryland

Monsignor Aidan Kempe, Father Tom Fenton, and Father Herm Volker sat stiffly across from the desk of the Cardinal Archbishop of Baltimore. Not even Kempe knew the reason for their curt summons. His expression betrayed mild contempt, while Fenton and Volker struggled to hide their anxiety. Such a peremptory order to appear at the chancery would leave most priests feeling unsettled, even fearful.

Cardinal Cullen was unreadable, which hardened Kempe's disdain but seemed only to heighten the anxiety in Fenton and Volker. Cullen hesitated. It appeared unclear, even to him, just how the conversation should begin, so he allowed the tension to build for a few extra heartbeats. It was only for a moment, but it worked to his advantage. Kempe grew impatient; Fenton and Volker, both ashen, stole an occasional glance at Kempe, who was seated between them. An unrepentant Kempe held Cullen's silent gaze.

"I am well aware," Cullen finally began, "that the three of you conspired together as members of a secret society, the Brotherhood of the Sacred Purple, along with a small number of other Baltimore priests. And I know that you, Monsignor Kempe, were the local leader of this society and personally reported to your grand master Pietro Montaldo, a Vatican bishop who just the day before his death was made a cardinal of the church. Your presence at the consistory, I must assume, was a tribute to his vision of the church, which—as you well know—I do not share.

"I mention all this, gentlemen, not because I care one whit what you believe about the church but because Cardinal Montaldo had in his employ a former carabiniere who served as his driver. His name is Giorgio Grotti. You, Monsignor Kempe, knew him under a different name when Montaldo sent him to Baltimore on the occasion of Archbishop Gunnison's golden jubilee. He was operating under the alias Monsignor Giancarlo Foscari."

Cullen waited a few seconds to give Kempe a chance to comprehend the depth of his exposure, but Kempe said nothing. He appeared to be irritated, even angry.

Cullen continued. "We know Grotti was the last person to see the archbishop before his untimely death. And we now have reason to believe that the last person to see Cardinal Montaldo alive was Giorgio Grotti."

Finally Kempe blurted, "Where's this all going, Charles? You should know...I was very clear about this...that the Brotherhood of the Sacred Purple was a simple fraternity of priests committed to keeping the church's sacred teachings safe from those who would dilute them with heresy. And you should likewise know that the Brotherhood of the Sacred Purple is no longer active."

Cardinal Cullen did not react to Kempe's surprising break in church protocol in calling him by his first name, but Fenton and Volker certainly did, both turning a deep scarlet. Kempe, showing no such compunction, moved to the edge of his chair and almost shouted, "So, *tell* us, Your *Eminence*, where's this all going?" The other two priests withered under Cullen's direct gaze, but Kempe stared straight at his superior.

"I understand the three of you returned to Baltimore on Monday, the day after Cardinal Montaldo's presumed fatal heart attack," Cullen continued in an even voice. "Is that correct?"

Volker and Fenton nodded meekly. Kempe grimaced at the word "presumed" but remained silent.

"So," Cullen continued, "you may not have heard that Montaldo's master of ceremonies, Father Trace Dunmore, was found dead in the episcopal palace of the Archbishop of Perugia. His body was found at the foot of a staircase. He suffered a broken neck...apparently in his fall down the steps." He paused to give his next words emphasis. "Or being thrown down a long staircase."

It was clear that the three indeed had not heard this news. Kempe's face turned gray, and a hint of panic glazed his eyes.

"Father Fenton and Father Volker," Cullen said, "let me give the two of you a little background that Monsignor Kempe may not have shared. Father Dunmore served for a short time as chancellor of the Diocese of Cleveland. He was a member of another small secret brotherhood formed by Cardinal Montaldo called the Sentinels of the Supreme Center, a rogue operation whose mission was similar to that of your now extinct Brotherhood of the Sacred Purple—the supposed safeguarding of the orthodoxy of the Roman Catholic Church from the forces of progressivism. They sought to accomplish this by arranging the execution of two irregularly ordained women priests and attempting the murder of the ordinary in Cleveland, Bishop Bryn Martin."

Fenton and Volker both instinctively stared at Kempe, hoping to hear him contradict the archbishop. Kempe never took his eyes from Cullen, and offered no defense.

"Now," said Cullen, drawing the noose tighter, "while we were at the Newark airport Tuesday we heard from the Vatican Police that Simon Ashley, Cardinal Montaldo's curator, was found dead—under a pew in the Cathedral of San Lorenzo, no less. Strangled, it seems."

Kempe's face was drawn tight, his eyes cloudy with confusion...or anxiety. Cullen wasn't sure.

"Two of Cardinal Montaldo's closest aides," Cullen continued, "two members of his episcopal household, turn up dead within forty-eight hours of the cardinal's death. One a tragic accident?" Cullen paused. "Personally, I don't buy it."

Fenton finally spoke up. "Father Volker and I only met Father Dunmore and this Ashley fellow at Cardinal Montaldo's reception in the Sala Regia. We spoke for just a few minutes."

Volker was silent, but nodded his head in agreement.

"You asked where all this was going, Monsignor Kempe," Cullen continued, ignoring Fenton. "A little patience, please. I'm getting there."

Motes danced in the afternoon sunlight falling harshly across Cullen's office. The room took on the atmosphere of a courtroom, or a judge's chambers.

"Let me return to Giorgio Grotti, better known to you as Monsignor Giancarlo Foscari." Cullen smiled inwardly. "The Carabinieri and the Vatican Police, the Gendarmerie, as you can imagine, are interested in interviewing him. Here's why. It looks like it was Grotti who turned on Montaldo's staff. Perhaps, even on the cardinal himself."

Kempe finally flinched. He was starting to get the picture. Grotti had always left him unnerved. He was one scary specimen, that was for sure. Maybe insane.

"Since you, Monsignor Kempe, were a known associate of Cardinal Montaldo, I thought you should know that these two other close associates of his are now dead. Now, my suspicion that Grotti was involved in their deaths is simply that, a suspicion. Even if my suspicions are true, his motives remain a mystery to me." Cullen paused. "That's not quite correct, I do have my own notions, but it would be imprudent to share them with you."

The silence that hung in the room after Cullen's remarks was palpable. He stood. "I think that about covers it, gentlemen." He gazed down at the three priests, still sitting as if frozen in their chairs, subdued at least, if not humbled, in his presence.

"Do the police have any idea where Grotti might be?" Kempe asked weakly, with a slight tremor in his voice as he rose from his chair.

"I don't believe they do. They have cast a wide net looking for him. But I guess a man with his background could be lingering just about anywhere."

Kempe closed his eyes, trying to calculate just how much danger he might be in. But the fear rising in his chest made clear thinking nearly impossible.

Rush hour traffic was just beginning when the three priests left the Catholic Center. They walked in stony silence to the Prime Rib on North Calvert. They sat at Kempe's favorite table with their drinks before them, still silent, processing Cullen's chilling revelations.

"Do you think *you* could be in danger, Aidan?" Volker asked clumsily.

"Of course I am," Kempe snapped. "Grotti must be out of his mind. And he knows six ways to kill you with his bare hands. I'm so angry I could kill the goddamn traitor myself. And all we know is that the police are 'looking for him.'"

"I doubt he'll come after you, Aidan," Fenton said, choosing his words carefully. "You're in a different position than Dunmore and Ashley. They saw him almost every day, they lived with him in his palace. You, on the other hand, had only a few personal meetings with Montaldo. I can believe he turned on the others, but I don't see why he would come halfway around the world after you."

Kempe sipped his twelve-year-old single malt. "I never mentioned this to either of you. I always felt that the less you knew about all this the better. But the night Wilfred Gunnison *officially* committed suicide, I provided Monsignor Giancarlo Foscari—that is, Giorgio Grotti—a key to the archbishop's hotel suite. Less than an hour later, Gunnison was dead."

"You mean Gunnison didn't commit suicide? You mean he was murdered?" Volker said, incredulous.

Kempe just stared at him. "Montaldo sent Grotti to talk Gunnison into leaving Baltimore immediately, maybe even leaving the country, right after his jubilee Mass and dinner. I told Montaldo that Gunnison's randy behavior with young boys was likely to come out in the media. But Gunnison vehemently disagreed. He felt confident that generous disbursements from the Purple Purse would continue to keep a lid on things. Then the Comiskey bitch outed Wilfred at his own celebration. Gunnison simply presented too great a threat to Montaldo's mission. He had to be eliminated."

Fenton and Volker sat stunned.

"I always believed Wilfred killed himself because he was outed," Fenton said.

"You see now why I'm worried that Grotti may view me as a threat. I know he was the last person to see Wilfred alive."

No one said a word...perhaps for a full minute. Kempe scanned the restaurant as if Grotti himself might be found lurking among the waitstaff.

"The damn shame is there's not a thing you can do," Fenton said.

"Until they nail this bastard, I'm going to hire a very good bodyguard." Kempe waved off the server approaching their table. "But a good bodyguard costs a lot of money."

Fenton and Volker nodded.

"As soon as I have the opportunity, I'm going to make a quick trip to Switzerland."

"Switzerland?" Fenton asked naively.

"I learned a lesson or two from Montaldo. Most of the money I funneled to him from the Brotherhood was deposited in a numbered account in Lausanne, Switzerland. So I opened another private account in the same bank."

"What if Montaldo had found out?" Volker asked.

"The cardinal was satisfied with what I sent him. Swiss banks are renowned for their discretion. There was no way he could ever have found out. So, about two thirds of what I collected from the Brotherhood and our conservative friends went to Montaldo, and a third went into a discretionary account under my name, for unforeseen emergencies of our own. It's time to close that account. I'll hire a bodyguard, maybe two, and I'll have the financial resources to do whatever I need to do."

He looked up into the shocked glares of his companions. "Don't you dare look at me like that," Kempe said with a menacing edge to his voice. I opened the account for the sake of the Brotherhood. I didn't want to rely entirely on Montaldo's largesse to underwrite our efforts here in Baltimore. It always remained a part of our Purple Purse, money we needed to keep the church right here in the U.S. orthodox."

Volker said, with a surprising new strength in his voice, "So you were skimming from our gifts, not just from the archdiocese."

"It was all for the Brotherhood, Herm. And to keep families who were claiming their children were abused from going to the press. Without money, the Brotherhood would have been more like the ladies of the Altar Guild—praying for an end to heresy in the church. You see that, don't you?"

Volker and Fenton exchanged a dark look.

"Enjoy your trip to Switzerland, Aidan," Fenton said coldly, tossing his napkin on the table and standing up. Volker stood as well and the two stalked out of the restaurant.

47

Nora Martin and Ian Landers sat across from each other at the same Charles Street restaurant in Baltimore where their relationship had first blossomed only a few years earlier.

"Are you sure you'll be up for your Secret Societies class tomorrow?" Nora asked.

"With a good night's sleep, I think it will go fine. How about you?"

"You handle jet lag better than I do, but I'll be okay."

"I've been thinking, Nora…how would you like to be a guest lecturer?"

Nora nodded interest, and Ian continued. "I'll be pushing things a bit tomorrow in the sense that I'll be slipping out of the Middle Ages. We'll be looking at the Illuminati who surfaced in the eighteenth century in Bavaria. And, if there's time, I'm going to do a sidebar on the Masons and the Italian Mafia."

"If you think I have something of value to add, sure, I'd be happy to do it. Not sure what I would say, though."

"You could address the psychological factors that make joining secret societies so attractive. Without naming him, you could use Giorgio Grotti as a case study."

"I've been thinking a lot about what exactly makes a person like him tick. My armchair analysis—that he is a gay man in deep denial—makes a lot of sense to me. Long term, semi- or sub-conscious denial, especially about one's sexual identity, leads to all kinds of intractable problems: lack of self-acceptance, a failed sense of integrity, things like that. Still, Grotti's apparent willingness to become an enforcer for a right-wing ideologue bishop intrigues me. Could it be that his bottled-up rage finds release in what he thinks is sacred vengeance? Sacred violence? He might even feel a kind of spiritual relief after completing one of his assignments. It's not too much of a reach to believe it was like that for Grotti."

"You're painting an intriguing clinical picture, Nora." He added a bit of white wine to their glasses. It was a dry malvasia he had long ago discovered in the walled medieval city of Orvieto, his favorite day trip when visiting Rome.

"So, yes, to your invitation, Ian. Let me know when I might fit into your class schedule."

"I can easily juggle the syllabus at this point in the course. I'll make it work."

Their entrees arrived. With their hearts still half in Italy, both Nora and Ian had opted for the evening's special, turkey tetrazzini.

"I spoke with my mother earlier today," Ian remarked.

"How is she?"

"She's fine. In fact, she'd been thinking a lot about Montaldo's death." Ian put his fork down and smiled. "The old girls enjoyed their rare peek into the dark side of the Vatican world. They'll be processing their Rome adventure for weeks, even months."

Nora waited, rightly suspecting that Ian was not just making small talk when he brought his mother into the conversation.

"You will no doubt remember that my cagey mother, the soft-spoken Ella Landers, was a foreign service professional before she retired. I also suspect, though she has never actually confirmed this, that she was CIA. Well, listen to this. She thinks that, yes, Grotti murdered Montaldo and wanted his death to look like a heart attack. She knows of no ingested poisons that would cause sudden cardiac arrest but would not be detected by routine postmortem toxicology. But an injection!" He lifted one index finger in the air as if just having made the discovery himself. "Her theory is that Grotti injected Montaldo, probably with a lethal dose of potassium chloride. That would have stopped his heart after a minute or two. She says that the cells of the body naturally shed potassium shortly after death, so a lethal dose could easily have escaped detection."

Nora shook her head. "Your mother never ceases to amaze me."

Ian smiled, sipped his wine, and said, "Me too. But there's more. Mother says that if the injection site was not in an obvious place—say in his foot—a medical examiner would very easily have overlooked the puncture."

"So an overweight man in his late middle years, found dead with no signs of physical trauma or struggle—"

"With movers and shakers in the Vatican pressing for a clean report."

"—could be easily determined to have died of a routine heart attack."

"Precisely."

Nora raised her glass. "To Ella Landers. The lady James Bond!"

48

Monsignor Aidan Kempe picked up the phone on its second ring. The caller ID read "The Catholic Center." He could feel his blood pressure rising.

"Monsignor Kempe?"

"Yes, this is he."

"Please hold, Cardinal Cullen wishes to speak with you."

"Hello, Aidan. This is Charles Cullen. Bishop Martin and I just received some information I wanted to pass on to you. We heard from the Vatican Police that Giorgio Grotti has been spotted in Lausanne, Switzerland. It looks like the police are closing in on him. Let's hope they get him soon."

Kempe felt a sharp chill of fright bolt through his body. "Lausanne?"

"Yes, it looks like he is on the run. I thought you should know."

Kempe took a deep breath. "Yes, it does look like he's running." An awkward pause followed before his dry lips parted. "Thank you for calling...Cardinal."

Kempe almost dropped the phone. An hour before Cullen's call he had made his flight reservations. BWI to JFK to Milan, then a short flight to Geneva where he would have rented a car for the one-hour drive to Lausanne...right into the arms of Giorgio Grotti! Kempe stood slowly, off balance with fear and confusion, and leaned over his desk. How he detested this heretic of an archbishop, now a cardinal. Charles Cullen had humiliated him, fired him as his financial secretary, accused him of fraud, and then exiled him to a tiny parish on the far side of the mountains. *Who knows what insult I might have to endure next?* He lifted his shoulders, closed his eyes, and finally had to admit to himself that Charles Cullen had probably just saved his life.

49

Charles Cullen pulled onto the curving white concrete driveway leading up to the eight-bedroom, six-bathroom home of Florence and Marcus Merriman, who were hosting an elegant cocktail party for about seventy major benefactors of the archdiocese. Cullen had been to their stately home three or four times before for fundraising events, but this evening's occasion was called to celebrate his new status as a cardinal of the Catholic Church. A few of the guests had travelled with them to the consistory, but most of the others had never met an actual cardinal.

Once Cullen had mingled sufficiently among the guests, Florence signaled the catering staff to leave. Lifting his voice and clinking his wine glass over the growing volume of small group conversations, Marcus said, "Good evening everyone, and welcome." The guests fell silent. "Florence and I are delighted that you could all be with us this evening to personally congratulate his Eminence, Cardinal Charles Cullen. A number of us here were privileged to travel with Cardinal Cullen to the consistory. It was, without exaggeration, a once-in-a-lifetime experience." He turned to Florence, who stood smiling at his elbow.

"If you can find a spot to put down your glass, let's applaud Cardinal Chares Cullen!"

Cullen nodded amiably as the wave of sustained clapping spread through the first floor of the spacious home. Or was it a bow?

As the applause waned, he said to the expectant crowd, "Thank you, thank you all. And special thanks to Florence and Marcus for hosting this very special event. I am so grateful for your friendship, and for your generous support of the archdiocese, Catholic Charities, our schools and seminaries, and our efforts to bring shelter and safety and dignity to the many men, women, and children of our region who are in real need. How deeply I appreciate your friendship. I mean that. As many of you know, I come from a working-class Irish family. I hope to God I will always remember my roots. It's pretty easy for someone like me to forget where I came from and lose sight of being a faithful priest and bishop. I need friends like you, who will speak to me frankly, tell me of your desires and fears and frustrations, your needs and hopes. As I continue to live and serve in your midst as your archbishop, now cardinal archbishop, I ask for your company...as fellow pilgrims...as friends. As your friend. I hope to always remain simply 'Charles' to each and every one of you. Thank you again. May God bless you...bless us all."

Florence raised her voice as a quiet round of applause died down. "Our 'friend' Charles has another engagement this evening, so he has to leave now." As she and Marcus walked him to the door, another round of applause rang out. Cullen turned and, with a final wave, left the party.

"While we still have your attention," Marcus said when the cardinal was gone, "Florence has something we think you should know."

"While arranging for the cardinal to join us this evening, I was on the phone a number of times with his secretary. His calendar, I'm sure you're not surprised, is really full. On one of these calls, I discovered where Charles is off to tonight. He asked his staff to arrange a spaghetti dinner for the maintenance personnel of all the local parishes, schools, agencies, and buildings of the archdiocese. He is going to personally greet each of them and thank them for the work they do for all God's people. And I'm sure he will ask them for their prayers." Florence had a second thought. "And let us say a prayer for all of them as well."

50

Professor Ian Landers stood chatting with Nora Martin in the front of the large, three-tiered classroom as the seventy-five undergrads in his Secret Societies of the Middle Ages course settled in their chairs. Landers glanced at the clock on the back wall. It was time to begin.

"Before we hear from our guest speaker, Dr. Nora Martin, are there any questions about our treatment of the Illuminati in our last class?"

"Dr. Landers," a girl named Chelsea said without raising her hand. "I might be confused, but I think you said the Illuminati's founder believed we could reach a state of perfection and be in communion with the divine by reason alone."

Landers nodded. "Right."

"Well to me," his student said, "the phrase 'achieving perfection and communion with the divine' sounds like a religion. Were the Illuminati a kind of religion?"

"Good question. The Illuminati's founder, Adam Weishaupt—and remember, it's spelled with a W but pronounced *Veishaupt*—had a Catholic education and was even educated by Jesuits. But he went all in with the Enlightenment. Weishaupt believed we could reach a state of moral perfection, as individuals and as a society, by reason alone. And by reason alone—here's where it gets a little tricky—we may find ourselves in communion with the divine. The Illuminati, you could argue, held to a kind of natural religion. There was no room for what Christians call grace, no need for sacraments or dogma, no need for divine revelation. Reason alone is enough of a light. But Weishaupt would be very emphatic about your point if he could come back from the dead and be our guest speaker." The students chuckled. "He would insist that the Illuminati were actually anti-religious in the sense of priestcraft and institutional religion. But perhaps our next speaker can illuminate all of us!"

Ian nodded at Nora, who joined him at the podium. "Dr. Nora Martin teaches in the Department of Health, Behavior and Society here at Johns Hopkins. The focus of this course has been the Secret Societies of the Middle Ages and beyond. We've wrestled with the difficulty in defining a secret society. Just what is it that lets us characterize a particular club, group, or organization as a secret society? There's a whole continuum of such groups. I'm afraid we will be wrestling with a precise definition right up to our last class. But today, Dr. Martin is going to help us look at what motivates an individual to join a secret society. Dr. Martin?"

Ian moved to an empty chair on the far side of the classroom.

Nora smiled, first surveying her audience as any good speaker habitually does. "It's a pleasure to be with you all this morning. My goal today is to explore why secret societies are attractive to such a large segment of people in most cultures and why secret societies have flourished throughout almost every period of human history."

Nora took a step forward and, tilting her head, said very softly, "Would you like to a know secret?" The students seemed to relax a bit in their chairs and a few of them smiled. "Of course you would say 'Yes.' Who doesn't want to know what others do not? Children, especially, love secrets. But no matter our age, we all seem to find that which is hidden to be alluring. And it feels good to be let in on a secret. To be one of the select.

"Children of all ages like to join with others in pursuing special objectives, or, just as often, ordinary objectives made to seem special. So when we combine 'secret' with 'society' we have a phenomenon that is quite powerful from both psychological and sociological perspectives. So, let's try to break that down."

Ian scanned the uplifted faces of his students. *You have them, Nora.*

"From a psychological perspective, I'm going to name a number of common human motivators that might help us understand why someone would be eager to be invited into a secret society or covert cult or exclusive organization. So here goes.

"Let's begin with emotional security. By that I mean that we need a sense of place, of belonging, of being sure we are known and accepted. It comes for most of us in our experience of family. But today, as in the past, a lot of people don't have that kind of personal, psychological security. Being a member of a secret society can meet that need.

"Now both psychologists and philosophers remind us that a sense of meaning or purpose is important for a healthy personal life. That's the second motivator. If your life is mainly about work and money, as it has become for a growing number of people in the developed world, then membership in a secret society might fulfill your need for a sense of meaning. It's a kind of secular transcendence. With a sense of meaning, life is no longer so one-dimensional, no longer routine or boring."

Nora paused. Most of the students were scribbling notes.

"In our postmodern culture it's easy to feel like you're a nobody. Just a number, a nugget of data, a no-name consumer. Just another brick in the wall. That's true for many, even if they're big time into Facebook. Commit to a secret society and suddenly you are a somebody! At least in your own eyes. A secret society, then, can give you a sense of identity, or strengthen a faltering sense of your own identity."

Nora moved to the whiteboard and block printed the words: SECURITY, MEANING, IDENTITY.

"The next motivating factor is a favorite of mine."

Nora went back to the whiteboard and printed the word: ROMANCE.

"I think a lot of us in our modern culture are starved for romance, and by 'romance' I don't mean the rush of falling in love. Romance, in the sense I'm using it here, means adventure, a great quest, a mighty undertaking, even an opportunity for personal heroism. Secret societies can give an individual just that—romance in the sense of a feeling of enchantment. Adventure in the sense of a certain kind of mild danger. Commit to a secret society and you will no longer find your life boring.

"The final motivating factor I'm going to mention is something Mr. Rogers told each of us: 'You are special.' And you are. You are indeed special. But here's the rub. If we fail to see that everybody else is 'special' in their own unique human dignity, we drift toward narcissism. You might grudgingly concede that other people are special, but you are *really* special." Her exaggerated tone drew a light laugh from the class. "We call this version of specialness exceptionalism. It means to have a compulsive need to be different from the crowd, to see ourselves as somehow extraordinary. Join a secret society and you will feel quite exceptional. Probably even superior to others who don't share the secret society's high sense of purpose."

Nora moved slowly across the front of the room.

"Even strong, independent, self-confident people may be drawn by the sense of power that comes with membership in a clandestine organization." Nora paused. "This can get pretty complicated. But then, things that motivate human behavior and personal choices always are."

She moved back to the board and added: SPECIAL and POWER.

"All right...any questions or comments?"

"So, Dr. Martin," the hand of a bearded young man shot up,

"are secret societies good or bad?"

"Well, that depends wholly on the intentionality of a secret society. In other words, what's the intention of the founder or founders of the society? The Ku Klux Klan, for example, fosters racism and has a history of terrible violence against those who don't represent the kind of white, Protestant America they believe is intended by God. Not good. Opus Dei, a Catholic secret society, intends to promote a spirituality grounded in orthodox belief and morality. Not bad in itself. But consider this. A lot of sociologists consider the early Christians to have been a secret society. Throughout the first three centuries of the Common Era, when Christians met with fierce persecution, followers of Christ behaved very much like members of a secret sect. Their survival depended on it. But overall, we should be wary of secret organizations. They tend to be elitist, and divisive, and subversive. Healthy societies are typically transparent and accountable. In other words, healthy societies, under normal circumstances and conditions, don't need to be secretive."

After a few more questions, Ian stood and moved toward the front of the classroom. "This was all very enlightening, Dr. Martin, thank you very much." The class clapped enthusiastically without a prompt. "Before you reach for your backpacks, here's something else to think about before our next class. Some historians believe the Jesuits are a secret society. And the Mormons, and of course, the Scientologists. So remember that much depends on not just the nature but the intentionality of any given secret society as well. The readings for our next class on the *Hashshashin*, the Assassins, are on the syllabus. Come prepared to see some blood spilled."

Nora walked Ian back to his office. The message light on Ian's phone was blinking as he put down his notes. He discovered a new voice mail and motioned Nora to one of the chairs across from his desk as he pressed the 'Play' button.

"Ian, this is Charles Cullen. Bryn just heard from Inspector Tosco that Grotti has been spotted in Lausanne, Switzerland."

Ian said, "Of course. The money."

"When you can, give me a call at the Catholic Center. Bryn will let Nora know. Tosco promised to keep us current with the effort to reel Grotti in. Talk to you later."

Nora had an idea. "We should have dinner with Charles. I think the consistory's really left him shaken. And there are only a few people he can talk to about it."

"Absolutely. It will be good for all of us."

Nora glanced at her cell phone. A message flagged "Urgent" was waiting for her from her brother.

51

Giorgio Grotti sat alone in the first-class lounge at Amsterdam's Schiphol Airport. Through the floor-to-ceiling windows he could see a bank of granite-blue clouds hanging low on the horizon, threatening a downpour. The weather fit his mood. Somber, and dwelling on gravely serious matters, careful calculations, and shrewd planning. He had enough privacy to make an important phone call to a woman of cunning and power. It was time to contact an old confederate, Mother Francesca, superior of the Immaculate Heart of Mary Convent and Retreat Center in Bogota, Colombia. He rehearsed the necessary coded exchange and then touched in the number to her private line. He would use Montaldo's code name, Murex. She answered after half a dozen rings.

"Mother Francesca?"

The voice at the other end of the call answered cautiously. "Yes."

"I am calling on behalf of Murex."

Grotti waited a few seconds for the coded response. Finally, Mother Francesca said softly, "May you be clothed in purple."

Grotti got down to business. "This is Monsignor Giancarlo Foscari."

"I remember you well, Monsignor."

"I'm afraid I'm calling with sad news. Our mutual benefactor, the Archbishop of Perugia, has passed away."

"I heard just a few days ago. May God's peace be with him."

"Once again, Mother, I am in need of your hospitality. I would like to come soon for a long retreat. As usual, your hospitality will be rewarded generously. I will bring your stipend with me. I will hand it to you personally when I arrive."

"Of course, Monsignor. You are always welcome here. I'll see to it that a suite is ready for you. When may we expect you?"

"Unfortunately, I can't give an exact arrival time just now. I have some urgent business to attend to in the U.S., but perhaps in a week or so. I'll call you the day before I arrive if that will be satisfactory?"

"That is quite satisfactory. I look forward to your visit."

A new chapter was opening in the life of Giorgio Grotti. His mission as a knight crusader defending the one true church would soon be concluded. That much was clear to him now. He would never have consented to Montaldo's offer had he known the man was a pervert, a pederast, *a man who buggered boys*. He hadn't thought of it before, but his last three assassinations had indeed been for the good of the church. He had only one more mission to complete before he could really rest.

Grotti stood and walked to the bar and asked for a glass of red wine. Avoiding eye contact with the bartender and the few travelers sitting at the bar, he promptly returned to his place in a quiet corner of the room.

He understood that he might be in some danger, but he more than felt up to the challenge of making the border crossings ahead. He took in a deep breath of cool air, stretching his legs out in front of him, satisfied with his plans. Monsignor Giancarlo Foscari would soon be safe in Bogota, tending to his lost soul with the sisters of the Immaculate Heart of Mary.

Grotti closed his eyes and mentally scanned his calendar. A little more than an hour remained before the boarding process would begin for his eight-hour Air Canada flight to Toronto. Then on to Maryland to take care of the loose end that needed a strong knot.

He dared not try to nap. Instead, he gathered his carry-on bag and headed to his gate. Across from his boarding area, a bookstore caught his eye. Flying with a book on his lap would discourage idle chatter from talkative fellow passengers.

Grotti picked up a copy of *Il Giornal* and strolled toward a colorful display in the section of the store labelled "Spirituality."

The pitch on the poster was in English and Dutch, hyping the work of "the Netherlands' Own Spiritual Master, Henri Nouwen." He had read some Nouwen as a seminarian, along with Thomas Merton, Léon Bloy, Thomas à Kempis, Therese of Lisieux, and the like. But he had missed reading Nouwen's *The Return of the Prodigal Son: A Story of Homecoming*. The haunting cover, Rembrandt's famous painting of the prodigal son from Luke's Gospel, stirred something deep inside the assassin.

He left the store with the newspaper and the book, a bit conflicted about his purchase of that particular title. With some difficulty he found a chair looking out on the crowded tarmac where fuel tankers and catering trucks were nestled under the wings or at the service doors of jumbo planes.

He glanced at the headlines of the *Il Giornal* and tried to hide behind its open pages. But he didn't really read a word. To help pass the time, he imagined his pending encounter with Monsignor Aidan Kempe. He had never liked Kempe. He remembered how the priest always smelled of cologne—a perfumed, French-cuffed clerical dandy in a tailored suit.

Kempe would look terrified, of course, when he understood the only possible reason for Grotti's presence. *What are you doing here?*

"Cardinal Montaldo would like you to join him."

But he's d—

"He wants to see you. You'll be with him very soon. *Vade in pace*, Monsignor."

52

Nora and Ian cleared the table after a simple dinner of meatloaf, mashed potatoes, and peas at the Silver Spring home of Ella Landers. They returned from the kitchen with carafes of coffee and tea. Nora went back to cut the pie she'd brought, lemon meringue, Charles Cullen's favorite.

"This evening is just what I needed," Margaret Comiskey said to the others while dinner settled. "I just wish Bryn could be with us."

Nora came in from the kitchen with five pieces of pie on a serving tray, just catching Margaret's lament. "So do I, Margaret. I miss my big brother."

Cullen sat coatless at the head of the table in a black clergy shirt, collarless and open at the neck. "This meal with dear friends is just what I needed, too. I'm still wiped from the consistory and the horrible drama that took all of us by surprise. I'm still shocked at the killings over there. It brought back all the pain and tension that Wilfred Gunnison's death brought down on the archdiocese."

"I've been noodling all this over," Ian said looking up from his dessert, "and I've concluded that Montaldo's scheme to save the church is something like a freak, fresh chapter of the Inquisition. But in this case, the self-appointed Montaldo is the grand inquisitor, the sole judge. He alone decided who was the heretic, who was the enemy of the church. He was the one man entitled to determine whether others lived or died."

"Wait a minute," Margaret interrupted. "You're saying heresy was not only a sin, but a crime?"

"That's exactly what I'm saying. A crime which, unless one recanted under torture, was punishable by death. Usually being burned at the stake."

"I'm shivering," Margaret said. "Why would a question of religious belief or non-belief be considered a crime?"

Ian held her gaze. "That's precisely why it's so critically important that we have a separation between church and state. When that distinction breaks down, decrying incorrect belief becomes an essential tool in maintaining order. Religious deviance, even doubt, becomes not only a sin, but a capital crime."

"What rationale did medieval popes give for murdering heretics?" his mother asked.

"Nora's heard this before, Mother—and forgive me if you have, too—but Montaldo's secret societies are nothing new in the church's history." He raised a napkin to his lips and gave them a few light pats. "There's a whole line of popes, from Gregory IX, to Innocent IV, to Alexander IV, who believed heretics were murderers of the soul. As such, they required the same punishment as murderers of the body—a very gruesome death—to persuade those tempted to doubt or dissent that they must repent and believe. And, most importantly, to submit."

Margaret shook her head. "I guess we've come a long way from the thirteenth century."

"You're right, of course, Margaret. We have come a long way. But here's a two-minute drill on just where we've come from. The sad story begins in 1231 when Gregory IX launched the first inquisition. Its target was a growing sect of Christians in southern France known as the Cathars. Thousands of Cathars—men, women, children—were put to death for their heretical belief in two Gods, one good, one evil."

"I need to hear this, Ian," Margaret said, putting her fork

down on the edge of her dessert plate.

"The second chapter began in the fifteenth century, the Spanish Inquisition. You might remember the name of the first Inquisitor General, the Dominican monk, Torquemada. Again, thousands of Christians were executed for crimes against the faith. Here's something almost no Catholics are aware of: The last execution of the Spanish Inquisition took place in 1826."

"Oh, my gosh! That's just a few generations ago," Margaret interjected.

"The year Thomas Jefferson died, as I remember," said Cullen.

"The heretic was a Spanish school master," Ian said. "In an apparent act of mercy, he was hanged by his neck rather than burned at the stake."

Ian pushed his plate of lemon meringue pie aside for the moment.

"There's a whole chapter we call the Roman Inquisition in which the church attacked the Protestant Reformation. The inquisitors focused on Protestants, but Jews, homosexuals, witches and miscreants in general were no less in danger."

Ella took a sip of tea. "And you haven't even mentioned the millions who died in the crusades."

"I'll save that lecture for our next gathering, Mother."

Cullen looked pained. "But to get back to your point, Ian. You're saying Montaldo may have thought of his personal vendetta against modernists and liberals as a righteous continuation of these earlier inquisitions."

"Exactly," Ian asserted. "That *is* my point. In fact, he probably thought he was taking the moral high ground by not subjecting *his* heretics to torture."

Margaret looked exasperated. "So the church authorities said you not only have to believe in Jesus, you have to believe in Jesus *correctly*."

"The same way they do, anyway," Nora said.

Ian nodded. "I'm afraid so. But let me finish with one sad 'first' in the church's history. The first man put to death by fellow Christians for incorrect belief was a priest. His name was Priscillian. He was a Spaniard. This was in 385. And we all know he was just the first of tens of thousands over the centuries."

The simple dinner to offer the new cardinal a chance to relax with friends had taken a grim turn. With a weary smile, Cullen said thoughtfully, "Thanks, Ian. Your guided tours into the church's past have always helped me immensely. Sometimes, I'm afraid, I take the easy way out. I tell myself we are, as we will always be, a church of saints and sinners. But we can't let ourselves become so complacent that we surrender to smug self-righteousness." Cullen shook his head. "We bishops ourselves are to blame for a lot of sanctimonious denial."

"Yeah," Nora said emphatically, "Hasn't denial become a staple of our ecclesiastical diet?"

"Ouch," Cullen winced. "Sure, our checkered history makes it clear to anyone that we are an evolving church, but we remain, at last, ever under the silent but powerful push of the Holy Spirit. We're not a static church. And we are as healthy as we are able to name our sins and ask for forgiveness for them. When I was in the seminary, church history courses seldom touched on the dark side of our faith tradition. We heard of the crusades and the inquisitions and the wars of religion, of course, but we glossed over the horror of them all—the injustices, the unremittent human suffering, the sinfulness. And we never heard a peep about the church's tolerance of slavery, even in the United States, or the forced conversions of colonized populations across the globe. It's so convenient to forget our corporate sinfulness. That's when we get puffed up with our own exceptionalism…the lofty notion that we alone are the one, true church."

"You know," Margaret said, "my imagination really took

flight that afternoon when Ella and I stood on the terrace of the restaurant looking down on the ruins of the Forum below us. I knew I was looking at the relics of a once great empire. A dark thought came over me then: What if, centuries from now, tourists to Rome will be drawn to visit the crumbled walls and roofless ruins of the Vatican?"

53

Henri Nouwen's *The Return of the Prodigal Son* touched a place in the soul of Giorgio Grotti that no one had ever touched before. He read the book, slowly, even prayerfully, straight through to the end. When he was done, he sat stone-still as a wave of emotion rose in his chest. He continued to sit trance-like for the remainder of the flight. He needed to remind himself that he was high over the Atlantic, flying to Toronto, flying—more like fleeing—from a world of vengeance and sacred retribution. And, of course, he was fleeing the jurisdiction of authorities who might want to question him about the deaths of Father Trace Dunmore and Simon Ashley, and maybe even the death of Cardinal Pietro Montaldo. But somewhere in all this fleeing, the assassin stumbled upon a sense of returning. Yes, a returning. But to what? And to whom?

A sudden jolt and the screech of the plane's tires on the runway brought him back to the moment. Grotti's balance seemed slightly off as he and his fellow passengers crept up the narrow aisle toward the plane's exit. After a moment he felt steady on his feet, and once off the plane moved with unstinting purpose to a quiet area of the terminal. There he reached for his phone and prayed his call would get through. For an instant, he thought his voice might crack. Mother Francesca answered after a few rings.

"I've cancelled my business in the States, Mother. So I will likely arrive sooner than I thought. You understand I have to move carefully. But I will come to your convent as soon as I can.

Perhaps in a week. I'll call you when I arrive in Bogota."

"Of course, Monsignor. There's no difficulty with your coming sooner than expected. Your rooms are already in order. I'll await your call, and we'll send a driver to pick you up."

Grotti slipped his phone into his right coat pocket with a deep wave of relief. He dropped into a nearby chair. He had a place to go, a convent retreat house, maybe even, eventually, a permanent home. He felt breathless and at the same time somehow weightless. He looked up at passengers moving with purpose toward their gates and others moving more slowly toward the baggage level. Grotti swallowed hard, and realized he was feeling something strange, something he hadn't felt since his childhood. He struggled to name it, and then it came to him: affection. That was it—*affection*—he was feeling affection for these total strangers.

After checking his suitcase in an airport locker, Grotti stood at the curb on the arrival level of Toronto Pearson Airport. There was a cacophony of annoying sounds—the poorly muffled engine roar of huge motor buses, whistles for taxis, the slamming of trunks and car doors.

"Taxi, mister?" a driver asked.

Grotti got in. "Take me to the nearest Catholic church."

"That would be Transfiguration. I'll have you there in five minutes once we get through this airport traffic."

Giorgio Grotti sat alone in a back pew of the Church of the Transfiguration. He was gasping for peace as if for air. His breathing turned slow and deep. He closed his eyes to the stained-glass windows, the statues, the altar, and sanctuary as if he couldn't tolerate the slightest visual stimulus. He drank in the stillness slowly, reverently, like someone drinking cool, sweet wine from a communion cup, sip after sip, until a calmness settled over him, embraced him. And in the silence, Grotti felt a presence. It was like…affection…a kind of unconditional acceptance. He felt like the prodigal son being welcomed home by the father who never stopped loving him. He understood now that he had been vainly searching for this presence all his life. When he was a seminarian, when he was in the Carabinieri, when he was an assassin for Pietro Montaldo, and now, as a penitent seeking the blessings of the sacrament of reconciliation.

Grotti opened his carry-on bag and took out Nouwen's book. He held it in his lap like a sacred relic, imagining Rembrandt's painting come to life. A moment passed before he slipped from the pew seat to his knees, whispering the words of the prodigal son: "I have sinned against heaven and against you. I'm not worthy to be called your son."

And the father said to Grotti, "You are my beloved son."

I was lost…and now I am found.

Epilogue

Giorgio Grotti, drawing on his training in the Carabinieri's elite Special Intervention Group, slipped easily enough into the United States. It took him two tedious days in a rental car to reach Dallas, where he boarded, without incident, a direct flight to Bogota, Colombia. His good fortune ended abruptly when he arrived in Bogota's El Dorado International Airport, however. As he moved from the baggage claim area he was greeted by three officers of Italy's Polizia di Stato. He was placed under arrest for the murders of Father Trace Dunmore and Simon Ashley, and led, with little ceremony, directly to a waiting Learjet 60, and a flight to Rome's Ciampino Airport.

Three months later, a contrite Grotti stood before an Italian judge for sentencing. He admitted killing Dunmore and Ashley. He also claimed to have had a subsequent spiritual awakening and asserted that in the light of it he had come to deeply regret taking the lives of the priest and the curator. It was reported in *la Repubblica* that Grotti told the judge he would accept the court's sentence as fitting penance for his sins. Giorgio Grotti was sentenced to thirty-one years in prison.

No connection between Grotti and the death of a Roman Catholic cardinal was ever made public.

Monsignor Aidan Kempe was adjusting poorly to the long, languid days of a country priest in the mountains south of Frostburg, Maryland. The unrelenting boredom sapped his energy, and the closest restaurant with a decent wine list was thirty miles away. If his external world was merely bleak, his interior life was one long, dark night of the soul. He wasn't sure what he believed anymore. He felt some relief when he heard of Giorgio Grotti's arrest. He stopped looking over his shoulder, thinking he was next in line after Dunmore and Ashley. But he still had to cope with another fear—that Grotti, from prison, might implicate him in the murder of Archbishop Gunnison. Kempe would never know on any given day whether there might be a knock on the door. The possibility alone was more than he could bear. He was too proud to indulge in self-pity, but in his life he had suffered one crushing disappointment after another. Had he not been destined to be a bishop? Was he not called by God to lead the Brotherhood of the Sacred Purple, to help promote the election of dogmatically sound bishops? And was he not anointed to save the church from the heresies of modernism, relativism, and liberalism? The fight was far from over, but he was nowhere near the front lines. Alone now, exiled in the backwaters of the archdiocese, without the friendship of even Thomas Fenton and Herman Volker, Aidan Kempe shuffled through each day like a bent old monk creeping along a dusty, parched path leading nowhere.

Cardinals Alessandro Oradini and Andrea Vannucci, recovered from the shock of Cardinal Pietro Montaldo's sudden death, slipped easily into their comfortable routines as princes of the church. Their principal entertainment, after leisurely lunches and dinner parties with the social elite of Rome and the Vatican, remained the inside politics of the curia. In this arena they remained preeminent masters, masters of secrets, those of others and their own.

Cardinal Charles Cullen spent most evenings that fall—when he wasn't at parish jubilees or confirmations—alone in his rectory listening to Bach, sipping a few fingers of single malt scotch, and trying to process the bizarre events surrounding the consistory that had bestowed on him his red hat. He often ruminated about the strata of corruption and infidelity that lay festering just below the grandeur of Saint Peter's Basilica, the Apostolic Palace, Bernini's colonnade. Anybody paying attention could see that. But he had seen it up close. Cullen knew that any institution of significant size would have its shadowy corners, hiding from public view the self-serving, power-seeking, money-grabbing agents of deception. But he had expected more from his beloved church's leaders. Most, of course, were good churchmen, and some even seemed truly humble. But more than a few were proud and self-seeking. He took some comfort in reminding himself that, despite attempts to obscure the simple truth of it, the church was not the Vatican or the Roman curia but the people of God. Church, like politics, was fundamentally local. And the church of Baltimore was in his care.

To help him remain mindful of this, Cullen had decided to create a kitchen cabinet. He tried to meet monthly with Ian, Nora, Ella, and Margaret. He prayed they would keep him honest and humble.

Bishop Bryn Martin stood at the window of his cathedral rectory suite in Cleveland, trying to read his own mood. The creeping buses and cars below slogged along as if themselves exhausted by a hard day's work. Then, in his own fatigue, he remembered a line from Thomas Merton that had always enthralled him. After a particularly dark day in the monastery, the spiritual master had lied to himself. Merton had whispered he "wasn't sad at all."

But Bryn Martin didn't want to repeat that lie. He was sad.

And it wasn't good to pretend otherwise. Things were not as they should be in his Catholic Church. Had they ever been? The question, Martin understood, was disingenuous. But he couldn't remember such dark clouds descending on his beloved church as were closing in now. Maybe five hundred years ago, with the corrupt Renaissance popes and the deadly religious wars spawned by the Reformation. But the present moment had its own particular darkness. The rape of young boys by priests and bishops, financial scandals at every level of church life, authoritarian clerics demanding doctrinal conformity and blind obedience to their own rigid morality. Yes, Bryn Martin was sad. His church continued to spurn the gifts and talents of its women. It had lost its moral authority in matters of marital sexuality, of sexuality itself. He could go on…

In spite of it all, Martin found rays of hope: Sister Celine's ministry to women caught in prostitution and sex trafficking; Sister Amelia and the brave leadership and witness of women religious; the largely uncelebrated but vital work of countless parish priests who continued their good work under the disdainful leer of an increasingly secular society; Catholic parents who trusted the power and mystery of grace and the life-giving spirit of their wounded church.

But sadness, like guilt, shouldn't be carried in one's heart. Sadness has its place, Martin understood, but when it floods the soul, it drowns joy. We have enough joyless shepherds. He thought of Aidan Kempe, a man incapable of laughter. He and so many others like him remained blind to the joy of the Gospel, just as they were blind to the joy of intimate friendship.

Martin's thoughts turned to Charles Cullen, to Ian, Ella, and Margaret, and especially to his sister, Nora. He couldn't help but smile.

Acknowledgments

Once I imagined a consistory as the setting for *The Cardinal's Assassin*, I needed to learn all I could about this rite of induction for Catholic prelates being raised to the College of Cardinals. To my good fortune, Archbishop Michael Fitzgerald, a visiting professor on the faculty of John Carroll University where I used to teach, had been raised by Pope Francis to the College of Cardinals in the fall of 2019. My hope that he would be helpful to me in understanding the ritual, structure, and protocols of a consistory was realized in abundance. With an amiability as charming as his humility, Cardinal Fitzgerald responded to each of my many queries with precision, clarity, and first-hand knowledge that proved immensely helpful in the writing of this novel. And all in a timely manner! Grateful beyond words for his gracious assistance, I dedicate *The Cardinal's Assassin* to Cardinal Michael L. Fitzgerald, M.Afr.

I am also grateful to Dr. Paul V. Murphy, professor of history and director of the Catholic Studies program at John Carroll University, for providing me with a detailed, comprehensive history of the Catholic Church's consistories.

The writing of the thriller you have just read required familiarity with the side arms and other weapons used by Vatican police and Rome's Carabinieri. I was aided in this area by former Secret Service Agent, Brian Dombek.

Getting away with murder is a major thread in *The Cardinal's Assassin*. Here I was greatly assisted and instructed by retired pathologist Dr. Phillip Catanzaro. I am also very thankful to both Brian Dombek and Dr. Catanzaro for their professional and technical expertise.

Readers of early drafts include Linda Catanzaro; Dr. Phillip Catanzaro; Mary Ellen Dombek; Daniel Dombek; Eileen Garven; Dr. Charles Garven; Marie Glasow; Timothy Glasow, Professor Mary Catherine Hilkert, OP; Dr. Richard Hofacker; Mary Ellen Lasch; Rick Porrello; John Scarano; Robert Toth; and Cathleen Walsh. Their feedback and encouragement generated energy for keeping me at my writing desk. My sincere thanks to each of them.

The Cardinal's Assassin, you might agree, reads as a lean, fast-paced story. To a great extent this is due to the experienced, incisive eye of my editor, Michael Coyne, and to the design and typesetting talents of Patricia Lynch. This is my third novel with ACTA Publications' publisher Gregory F. Augustine Pierce, who suggested that my first story, *Master of Ceremonies,* might find a home with ACTA's imprint, In Extenso Press. It did indeed. I'm grateful to Michael and Patricia and Gregory for their critical insights that shaped and sharpened this final novel in the Bishop Bryn Martin murder mystery trilogy.

ECCLESSIAL NOVELS
FROM ACTA PUBLICATIONS

MASTER OF CEREMONIES
Donald Cozzens

UNDER PAIN OF MORTAL SIN
Donald Cozzens

THE CARDINAL'S ASSASSIN
Donald Cozzens

DEATH IN CHICAGO
WINTER
Dominic J. Grassi

PISTACO
A TALE OF LOVE IN THE ANDES
Lynn F. Monahan

ACTA PUBLICATIONS
800-397-2282 • www.actapublications.com
actapublications@actapublications.com